PAT RANDOLPH missed John terribly. Sooner or later they would work out their differences. Maybe Barbara could help . . .

BARBARA WEAVER'S feelings for John had always been under control. He was married. But all that was different now, or so he said. Could she believe him?

JOHN RANDOLPH loved Pat. He didn't want to lose her, but he also couldn't resist his increasing fascination with Barbara, his gorgeous legal associate. He was playing a dangerous game.

———————————

Series Story Editor **Mary Ann Cooper** is America's foremost soap opera expert. She writes the nationally syndicated column *Speaking of Soaps*, is a major contributor to soap opera magazines, and has appeared on numerous radio and television talk shows.

Martha Winslow is the pseudonym for a novelist and television writer who lives in New York City.

Dear Friend,

Our offices have been buzzing with excitement lately. Can you guess why? We're compiling material for our newest Soaps & Serials books.

Pioneer is proud to announce the addition of three outstanding shows to the Soaps & Serials line:

GENERAL HOSPITAL
ALL MY CHILDREN
ONE LIFE TO LIVE

We'll be introducing these new releases with a festive splash. Look for them! And don't miss our new and exciting features in forthcoming Soaps & Serials books.

For Soaps & Serials books,

Mary Ann Cooper

Mary Ann Cooper

P.S. If you've been searching for previous volumes of Soaps & Serials books and can't find them in your local book source, please see the order form inserted in this book.

ANOTHER WORLD

10

DECEPTIONS

PIONEER COMMUNICATIONS NETWORK, INC.

Deceptions

ANOTHER WORLD paperback novels are published
and distributed by Pioneer Communications Network, Inc.

SOAPS & SERIALS™ is a trademark of Pioneer
Communications Network, Inc.

ISBN: 0-916217-40-X

Printed in Canada

10 9 8 7 6 5 4 3 2 1

DECEPTIONS

Chapter One
A New Romance?

With a glance at his desk calendar and another at his watch, John Randolph picked up his phone to call Bay City Memorial Hospital. Then he paused, frowning as he cradled the phone. Hospital switch-boards never told a person anything, sometimes even neglecting to mention that the patient inquired about had died. If he really wanted to know how Rachel Cory was getting along he'd have to call her doctor.

He picked up his phone again but did not dial. The trouble was, Rachel's doctor was Dave Gilchrist, and Dave Gilchrist was the last man in the world to whom he wanted to speak. He cradled the phone again, pushed back from his desk, and went to stand at the window overlooking the street below. After a rainy, drizzly day, the late afternoon sun was trying to break through the clouds for a final weak blaze before going down.

With a sigh he turned from the window and went back to sit at his desk. His eyes rested on the framed portrait of his family—his wife, Pat, and the twins, Michael and Marianne, and himself. John shook his head. He shouldn't really blame Dave Gilchrist for his part—or non-part—in Marianne's recent troubles, but nevertheless he did. The least Dave could have done was to tell him what was going on, what Marianne was going to do. But John had been kept in the dark until it was all over and done with, and even then he discovered what had happened only by accident.

John shook his head again as if trying to clear his mind. He couldn't spend the rest of his life avoiding Dave Gilchrist. After picking up the phone, he resolutely dialed the doctor's office, and the office nurse put him through.

"Yes, John," Dave said, coming on the line, speaking as though there'd never been a harsh word between them. "What can I do for you?"

"I'm calling to ask about Rachel Cory," John said. "I'd like to go see her if she's up to it."

"By all means."

Surprised at the response, John arched his eyebrows. "Is she that much better then?"

The tone of voice this time was more equivocal. "No, not that much. But she's up to seeing people —if they don't stay too long."

"I won't do that," John said.

"No, I'm sure you won't. And while I've got you on the line, John, tell me about Pat. Have the two of you thrashed things out yet?"

John turned in his seat to glare at the picture of his wife. This was precisely why he hadn't wanted to call Dave. "No, we haven't, Dave, and I don't want to talk about it."

"Look, she was only trying to—"

John cut him off. "I said I didn't want to talk about it, and I meant it. Thanks for the information about Rachel, and I'm sorry to have bothered you. Good-bye." Without waiting for Dave to answer, he broke the connection. He tucked the phone into his shoulder and reached for the phone book to look up and dial the number of the florist in the lobby downstairs.

While the phone rang at the other end, he thought about what flowers to take to Rachel. Carnations. He loved their spicy smell. When the florist came on the line he ordered a dozen red ones. "I'll pick them up in a few minutes on my way out of the building," he said.

"Right, Mr. Randolph," the florist answered. "I'll have them ready for you."

"Thanks," John said, and once again he cradled the phone, lost in thought.

Who would have ever believed he would be taking flowers to Rachel? He considered all the damage she had done only a few short years ago, first to Pat's brother Russ Matthews, then to their sister Alice, and to Steve Frame—to all the Matthews family really, including his own wife. Still, times change, and so do people, and Rachel had come a long way from the money-hungry schemer she once was, heedless of anybody's feelings or well-being other than her own.

Those same few short years ago, if anybody had

told him he would one day have reason to be grateful to Rachel, he would have told that person to go have his head examined. Yet he was grateful to her. After his big fiasco with Steve Frame, when he'd nearly lost everything to drinking, Rachel was the one who'd helped him dry out and regain his self-respect. And Rachel was the one who had interceded for him with Pat, enabling them to get back together.

But now they were estranged again. And this time he didn't know of anybody who could make things right between them. Or even if things could be made right again. He was beginning to believe it wasn't possible.

The sound of ruffling papers made him look up. His associate, Barbara Weaver, was standing in front of his desk, a sheaf of papers in her hands.

John felt his eyes widen in surprise, and when he spoke, surprise was in his voice as well. "Where did you come from?"

Barbara smiled. "I came in through the door. You were miles away, that's all." She was a tall, shapely blonde, so attractive one would think he'd hired her to decorate the outer office instead of for her brains and ability as a lawyer. Her bright smile lit up her flawless facial features.

He returned her smile. "Yes, I guess I was. What can I do for you?"

She held the sheaf of papers out to him. "Tell me if this is what you had in mind, more or less, as far as the courthouse business is concerned."

He took the folder and started leafing through the papers. The "courthouse business," as they had come to call it, was a class action suit he was bringing to trial on behalf of a group of employees at the county courthouse who had been kicking back two percent of their salaries to the local Boosters Club for years and who had grown tired of doing so. He had asked Barbara to research some similar cases that had been brought to trial in other states.

"It looks fine to me," he said, handing the folder of papers back to her. "Were you able to find any material on that case that was tried three years ago in North Dakota?"

Barbara gave him a curious look, one he couldn't figure out until she spoke. "It's in there. Didn't you see it?"

Sighing, he held out his hand for the papers again. "No, I guess I didn't. Look, leave them with me overnight, okay? I'll take them home with me and really read through them. There's too much distraction here in the office."

She raised an eyebrow, smiling wryly. "Here in the office or there in your head?"

"Right again," he said, chuckling. He put the folder down and leaned back in his chair, waving her to a seat on the other side of his desk. "Talk to me."

"What about?"

He shrugged. "Anything. The price of eggs. Who's doing what to whom. Grain futures. The stock market. The latest trend in women's fashions." He spread his arms. "Anything."

She studied his face. "What's bugging you, John?"

He paused before speaking. "My marriage. Or I should say my non-marriage."

"Do you mean that, when you say non-marriage?"

He nodded. "I think so. Yes."

Barbara frowned. "All those years together, and it's over"—she snapped her finger and thumb —"just like that?"

He hesitated again before answering, then said, "I'm not sure all those years together, as you put it, were really that."

Her frown deepened. "And I'm not sure I follow you."

John picked up a ballpoint pen and rolled it between his fingers. "What I'm trying to say is I don't think my wife ever really loved me."

"I find that hard to believe, John." She shook her blond head. "If Pat didn't love you, why did she marry you?"

"Gratitude," he said at last.

This time Barbara didn't dispute him, but she didn't look convinced either.

"Look," he said, rising and coming around the desk to lean against the front of it, "haven't you ever been grateful to somebody for something? To a man, say?"

She considered, then her face cleared. "Yes. To one of my professors in law school. He saved me from making a terrible mistake. I was very grateful to him."

"Okay, then, tell me this. Didn't it make such a glow in your heart you almost felt you loved him?"

She nodded. "Yes, you're right. I did."

"Well, then? Do you see what I mean?"

"Yes, I guess I do," she said, frowning. "But with you and Pat, surely there was more to it than gratitude for clearing her name. I'm assuming you're talking about when you represented her in that trial."

"Yes, that's what I'm talking about. And yes, there was more to it than that. The man she was accused of murdering, the man she'd been in love with, was no more than a boy—emotionally immature as well as young. He was conceited, totally absorbed in himself, and completely indifferent to Pat's welfare. When she put that up against me, what did she see? Somebody who was older, established in his career, secure." John shook his head. "Any way you look at it it was a winning combination. And to Pat, vulnerable as she was, extremely grateful as she was, her parents singing my praises —well, it all added up to what she thought was love."

"I suppose so," Barbara said quietly.

"I'm sure of it," John said. "Otherwise we wouldn't be where we are today. And where, I might add, we've been before."

Barbara examined his face again, her gaze meeting his own. "Then your marriage really is over, John?"

"Yes," he said. "Over and done with." He gave her a wry smile. "So much for being older, established, and secure."

The smile Barbara gave him in return had no wryness to it at all. "There's more to it than that," she said. "You're leaving out handsome and sensitive and thoughtful and—" She broke off, color suffusing her fair skin. "But never mind that." She got to her feet, the color deepening in her face, and turned to leave the office. Then, just as abruptly, she turned back to him, took one of his hands in hers, held it to her face, then kissed it.

John stared at her in astonishment, but before he could gather his wits together to say something, she had turned away from him again, and this time she half ran out of his office and into her own, shutting the door after her with a sharp snap.

He put the hand she had kissed to his face, rubbing his cheek, staring after her, still astonished. He had had no idea she had this kind of feeling toward him.

He waited for her to come out of her office. When she didn't, he went after her, was about to open her office door when he stopped, telling himself maybe she hadn't really meant to do what she'd done, was maybe already regretting her impulsiveness, in which case his pursuit of her would only be a further embarrassment to her.

Retreating to his own office, he stuffed the papers she had given him into his briefcase, grabbed his raincoat, and headed down to the lobby to pick up the carnations for Rachel.

Chapter Two
Lies

While John Randolph was driving to the hospital, another visitor was entering Rachel's room—the stunningly beautiful, blond ice-princess, Iris Cory Carrington Delaney. At one time—when it had suited Iris's purpose—Rachel had been her ally. Then Iris had become indifferent to her. But after Rachel had had the audacity to marry Iris's multi-millionaire father, Mackenzie Cory, Rachel had become the enemy. And so she remained.

Indeed it was Iris who was most to blame for the miscarriage Rachel had suffered a few days ago. Taken aback—to put it mildly—by her father's grief at the loss, fearful of what would happen if he ever learned the truth, Iris had since been doing all she could to erase any suspicion of her. And now that Rachel was finally able to have visitors, Iris was there to finish covering her tracks.

She came into the room prepared to give Rachel a warm and compassionate greeting, the better to set her up for what was to follow, but at the sight of the flowers covering the bedstand and windowsill, bouquet after bouquet after bouquet, she stopped dead in her tracks, too stunned to speak.

Then she caught herself. It was just like her father, of course. She should have known. And especially typical of him when he felt that he was to blame for something. Do something magnanimous. Shower Rachel with flowers. Overwhelm her with them. That would prove how sorry he was that he hadn't been with her when the first pain struck, that he hadn't reached home in time to keep her from losing the baby.

Iris turned to Rachel with a knowing smile. "How like my daddy, isn't it?" she said by way of greeting.

Rachel gave her a confused look. "I don't know what you mean."

Iris waved an imperious hand. "All these flowers he sent you."

Half propped up in bed, pillows cushioning her back, Rachel had her dark hair loose about her heart-shaped face, the strain of her suffering still showing in the whiteness of her skin. She raised a hand and let it fall again. "They're not all from Mac. The red roses are from him. The others are from other people."

"Oh," Iris said, and walked over to the flowers on the windowsill to see for herself. The first card read, LOVE FROM MOM, GIL, AND NANCY. Well, of course. She would expect Rachel's family to send flowers. Another card was from Pat Randolph. Another from Stan and Ella, whoever they were.

Another from Henry, whoever he was. She stopped looking at the cards. It was all too depressing.

Rachel gave her a weak smile. "And thank you for the tulips you and Robert sent."

About to say "What tulips?" Iris caught herself and turned to look at the magnificent bouquet of red, white, and yellow tulips taking up most of the bedstand's surface. Anger flared up in her. The least her husband could have done was tell her he was sending them. Instead he had come close to making a fool of her. Which, she thought bitterly, was no doubt what he had intended.

She smiled stiffly. "You're more than welcome, Rachel."

She had barely finished speaking when a nurse's aide came into the room with a vase of yellow chrysanthemums. After rearranging some of the other flowers to make room for the new arrival, she took the envelope and handed it to Rachel, saying, "If this keeps up you'll have to open a flower shop." Then with a bright smile at Iris, who glared at her with scorn, she left the room.

Rachel opened the envelope and read the card. "They're from Clarice."

"How nice," Iris lied, and thought to herself that the timing of that gift had probably been deliberate, too. But she was not going to get into that with Rachel now.

Apparently Rachel felt the same way, because she put the card with the others and said no more about the sender. What she did say, however, was almost as aggravating to Iris. "It *is* quite a lot of flowers, isn't it?"

"Yes," Iris agreed. "It is."

Rachel had long had a habit of sticking out her chin in a gesture of defiance, and she did it now. "I bet you didn't know I had so many friends, did you, Iris?"

"No, Rachel, I didn't." And she hadn't—any more than she had known, when Rachel called the other night looking for Mac, that she was on the verge of a miscarriage. Swallowing, she said, "It must be a great comfort to you."

At this reminder of why the flowers had been sent, the little show of spirit faded from Rachel's dark eyes. "Yes," she said listlessly, "it is."

Giving Rachel's hand a solicitous pat, Iris drew a chair up to the bedside and sat in it. "Now, darling, you mustn't let yourself get depressed. It's very sad what happened, and I know how bad you feel, but it could have been worse. At least you're going to be all right."

Rachel nodded.

"And you can always have another baby."

She nodded again. "Yes. I know."

"And you do still have Jamie, and he's such a lovely young boy."

Rachel brightened. "Yes, he is, isn't he?"

Iris squeezed Rachel's hand. "Of course he is. Everyone says so."

As if that had been timed as well, the phone at Rachel's bedside rang. It was Jamie, calling to ask after his mother. Iris settled back in her chair, only half listening to the conversation, struck more by the tone and timbre of Rachel's voice and the tiredness settling in her eyes, despite her obvious attempt to be "up" for Jamie's sake. When the call was finished, Rachel hung up the phone with a sigh. "I can't seem to get my strength back," she said. "The least little thing exhausts me."

"I don't wonder," Iris said. "When you think of what you've been through. And especially the fever. That's so debilitating, don't you think?"

Iris doubted that she knew what the word debilitating meant, but Rachel nodded and said, "Yes, it is," probably figuring that was the response called for. For the umpteenth time Iris asked herself what in the world her father had ever seen in Rachel, and wondered what she could do to make him understand that this was a disastrous marriage, the sooner ended the better?

The trouble was, her father was just as dazzled now by Rachel as he ever had been. She would never have believed that her father, so intelligent, so powerful, so wonderful a man could have been swept off his feet by this selfish, money-mad, unrefined little nothing. It was unbelievable. And even more unbelievable that he hadn't yet wised up to her. Iris shook her head.

"What's the matter, Iris?" Rachel said.

Iris looked at her in surprise. "The matter? What do you mean?"

"You were shaking your head over something."

"Oh." She hadn't realized she'd done that. She was going to have to be more careful around Rachel. Especially from here on out. Rachel might be a little on the ignorant side, but she had that shrewdness so many basically uncultivated people had. Iris smiled. "I was thinking about you, Rachel, and how sorry I feel for you. I mean, I've never had a miscarriage, but I know how I would feel if anything ever happened to Dennis. The same as you'd feel, I'm sure, if anything happened to Jamie." She held up a hand. "Now that was a stupid thing for me to say. Nothing is going to happen to Jamie. Or to Dennis either. Please forget I said anything at all."

"It's all right, Iris," Rachel said. "I know what you meant. I appreciate that."

"I hope so, darling." Iris ran a finger along the narrow pleat of her navy blue skirt. "And there's something else I want to ask you to forget." She gave her a brighter smile than before and waited for her to make a response.

Dutifully Rachel said, "What, Iris?"

"That terrible dream you had. Or hallucination, I think the doctor called it."

Rachel frowned. "You mean about my calling your house looking for Mac?"

Iris nodded and pinched the pleat between her fingers. "Yes, Rachel, that's exactly what I meant. Because it was only a dream, you know."

Rachel gave a weak sigh. "But it seemed so real. I remember I—"

"Not remember, Rachel," Iris said, cutting her off. "You can't remember doing something you never in fact did."

Rachel sighed again. "All right. But it seems to me—" She broke off and turned to look at Iris. "Is it all right if I say that?"

Iris gave her an understanding smile. "Yes, of

course. And do talk to me about it. That will help get it out of your system."

Rachel nodded uncertainly. "I'm so sure—I mean—I could have sworn—" She broke off again and for a few moments said nothing. She settled back on the cushions as if stalling for time while trying to figure out exactly what to say.

Iris didn't prompt her. She simply waited.

Eventually Rachel began speaking again. "It just seems to me I went to the phone and called you. I can see—" She broke off again and swallowed. "I mean, I knew Mac was at your place. He had called me earlier to ask me if it was all right with me if he stopped off to see you on his way home."

Iris nodded. "Yes, I know that. He told me he'd called you. So that part of it is true."

"It seems to me," Rachel said, "that all of it is true. The two things aren't any different inside my head."

Mentally, and she made sure it was only mentally, Iris frowned. Apparently this was going to be harder to do than she had thought. Outwardly she smiled encouragingly. "But that's because of the fever."

Rachel gave her a dull look. "What's because of it?"

"That the two things, as you put it, aren't any different inside your head. Because of the fever everything is all mixed up. You think Mac called you to ask if he could stop off at my place—"

"But he did call me," she cut in with a frown. "You just said he did."

"Yes, my dear. I know I did. If you'll just bear with me, I'm trying to demonstrate something to you."

"Oh," Rachel answered, looking confused.

"And you think you called Mac at my place to ask him to come home, that it was urgent."

Rachel nodded. "And I did. Honest, Iris, I did call him. I remember—" Breaking off, she covered her face with her hands. "I could have sworn I did," she said in a despairing voice.

"It's the fever," Iris repeated soothingly. "Mixing things up inside your head. Darling, look at it this way. If you had in fact called me looking for Daddy, wouldn't I have sent him home to you?"

Rachel was pleating the sheet covering her as Iris had been doing with her navy skirt. "I guess so," she said.

"Well, of course I would have. Especially when you said it was so urgent. What reason would I have had not to send him?"

Rachel shook her dark head listlessly. "I don't know."

Iris leaned in toward the bed. "Then you must believe me. You didn't call me. You only think you did. Maybe you had wanted to. That's probably it. When the pain first started, you said to yourself, I must call Iris and get her to send Mac home, because I need him." She nodded in satisfaction. "You may even have started toward the telephone. You probably did, thinking as you went to it that you had to hurry, the pain was getting worse, it might be something serious. Mac would know, and he would certainly get help." Iris continued to nod reassuringly. "But then before you could get to the phone you collapsed on the floor. Where my daddy found you when he did get home. Lying on the living room floor on your way to the phone to call me to ask for him. That must be what happened, Rachel."

Rachel sighed. "I guess so, Iris. If you say so."

Iris put one hand behind her back and crossed her fingers. "Darling, I wouldn't want to put words into your mouth. I'm only trying to make sense out of what actually happened, and what actually happened was you didn't call me."

"All right."

Iris leaned closer. "You do believe me then?"

"Yes, Iris. I believe you." Another sigh. "I have to believe you. Either I did call you or I didn't, and you say I didn't, so what else can I believe?"

Iris sat back in her chair, allowing herself an inner smile of triumph. It hadn't been so difficult after all. And best of all, should Rachel go back to saying she didn't just dream she'd made that phone call, it was Iris's word against Rachel's, and Iris hadn't been sick or had a fever to cast doubt on her contention.

There was, of course, a witness. Tracey. But she had promised to keep silent about that evening, and Iris was sure she could count on her.

Leaning toward the bed again, Iris said, "Rachel, I don't want to overstay my welcome. The doctor said not to let you get too tired."

Rachel waved a limp hand at her. "It's all right, Iris. I'm okay."

"Yes, but you won't be if I don't get out of here and let you rest. I'll come back again tomorrow."

"All right."

Iris covered the limp hand with her own cold one. "Take care, darling. And enjoy those flowers."

The good-byes over, Iris left the room, smoothing her navy skirt, checking the collar of the matching jacket to see that it lay smoothly against her neck. Halfway down the corridor she ran into John Randolph, presumably on his way to Rachel's room.

They exchanged greetings, and anybody seeing and hearing them would have assumed they had a cordial relationship. But Iris had never cared for John, and her feeling of triumph at having bested Rachel was somewhat marred when she saw the red carnations in his hand. Here was yet another floral contribution for that money-grubbing little tramp.

With an audible sniff Iris continued on her way. What did she care if John Randolph wanted to cater to Rachel? He had never meant anything to Iris, and furthermore he never would.

Which showed how little Iris knew.

From what Dave Gilchrist had said on the phone, John hadn't expected to see Rachel up and about and clamoring to go home. But neither had he expected to see her looking so white and drained.

He strode to the bedside. "Are you okay, Rachel?" he asked without first greeting her.

She nodded.

He wasn't convinced. "Let me call a nurse. Or

what about Dr. Gilchrist? Maybe I ought to call him."

Rachel put a hand out to take hold of his wrist. "No, John, please. I'm okay. Really I am. It's just that Iris Delaney was here."

"I know," he put in. "I ran into her in the hall."

"And she's a little hard to take, that's all."

John frowned down at her. "Was she giving you a hard time about something?"

"Iris wouldn't call it that," Rachel said, smiling weakly.

John's frown deepened. "Is it something I can help you on?"

"No, I'm afraid not. It isn't something anybody can help me on. But let's not talk about it, okay?"

He nodded. "Whatever you say, Rachel. Here." He held out the carnations. "For you."

Her smile brightened. She took the flowers and held them to her nose to sniff their fragrance. "They're one of my favorite flowers—carnations. They smell so delicious."

John laughed. "I have to confess that's why I chose them. Let me put them in a vase for you." He looked around. "My Lord, you're surrounded by flowers."

"I know. Even Iris was impressed—after I explained to her that they didn't all come from her father."

Hunting for a vase, John searched the tiny closet next to the bathroom. "Is that what she thought?"

"Yes. Look up on that shelf, John. I think there's one there."

Finding the vase, he reached for it, then took it into the bathroom and filled it with water. He brought it back to Rachel, arranging the carnations in it as he did so. He set the vase down next to the chrysanthemums, then came around the bed to sit in a chair already pulled up beside it.

"That's where Iris was sitting," Rachel said.

John laughed again. "I'll try not to let it rub off on me."

"Then, you don't like her either, do you?"

"No way. Not that I've seen that much of her. Or had anything at all to do with her other than be a guest at the same dinner party." He shook his head. "But from what I've seen of her, she strikes me as selfish and spoiled and not above using anything or anybody to get her own way."

"That's putting it rather precisely," she said, smiling warmly.

"Yes," John agreed. "Like a hatchet making short work of a piece of wood."

"Oh, dear," Rachel said, laughing. But the laughter abruptly turned to tears.

John was alarmed at this outburst. "Rachel," he said, leaning toward her. "What is it?"

She reached for a tissue to wipe her eyes. "Nothing, John. I'm okay. It's just that, well, it was so good of you to come see me and to bring me flowers. And it was so nice of all these other people"—she waved a hand toward the windowsill —"to send me all these lovely flowers. And I can't help thinking what it was like when Jamie was born." She swallowed and wiped her tears. "I didn't have a friend in the world."

John reached out to pat her hand. "Oh, now, Rachel, it wasn't that bad."

Weakly she shook her head. "You're only saying that to make me feel better, but you know I didn't." Again she swallowed. "And I didn't deserve to have any either."

John cast about for something to say, but all he could come up with was another, "Oh, now, Rachel."

It was apparently enough to soothe her. She tried a smile and said, "But that's all behind me, isn't it?"

"Indeed it is. Long behind you."

"And all because of Mac. He made me the person I am today." Fresh tears welled in her dark eyes. "And we both wanted this baby so much."

John squeezed the hand he had been patting. "I know, Rachel. I know. Life can be hard sometimes. But try not to think about it."

She squeezed his hand in return. "I know. Because it can't undo what's been done." She sighed, then shook her head as if to shake off what she had been thinking. "Did I thank you for the carnations you brought me?"

He smiled. "I'm sure you did."

"You needn't have brought me anything, you know. Pat sent those flowers over there." She pointed to an arrangement on the windowsill of mixed spring flowers—tulips, daffodils, and some wildflowers he couldn't name.

"Very pretty," John said. "Very tasteful." But then Pat had always had good taste about everything. A stab of longing shot through him. Maybe he was being too harsh with Pat, too intent on simply wanting to punish her for what had surely been no more than a mistake in judgment. Yet how could she have made such a mistake? If she had really had his welfare uppermost in her mind, wouldn't she have shared with him what Marianne was up to? He sighed. Then shutting his mind to thoughts of Pat he said to Rachel, "When is the doctor going to let you out of here?"

"I don't know," she answered. "I have to get stronger first. I have to get over being so tired."

John got to his feet. "And that's my cue to get out of here. Your doctor warned me about overtiring you."

She grabbed his hand. "Oh, don't go. You just got here. Please."

"A couple more minutes, then," he said, but he remained standing.

"Tell me about you and Pat."

He shook his head. "I'm afraid there isn't anything to tell you."

Rachel frowned. "Then you're still not back together?"

"No."

"But you are still talking, aren't you?"

"More or less."

She was looking intently at him—almost, he felt, as if she could read his thoughts. "But sooner or later you will get back together, won't you?"

He shrugged. "I don't know."

"Oh, dear," she said. "I don't like the sound of that."

"I don't mean to upset you, Rachel. Nothing is definite."

She squeezed his hand and smiled at him. "Well, that's some comfort."

He put his other hand up in a warning gesture. "But nothing is definite on that side either."

"I understand." Nodding, she squeezed his hand again. "John, let me help you like I did before. Let me talk to Pat."

"No, Rachel. Not," he added hastily, "that I don't appreciate your offer. But the situation is a little different this time. And anyhow you can't be concerned now about other people's problems. You've got to concentrate on getting well."

"I could do both."

"No, I can't ask that of you. Not now."

She was looking at him intently again. "Can't ask it or don't want it?"

He returned her gaze with an intent look of his own. "Do you want an honest answer?" When she nodded, he said, "Then I don't know which it is, Rachel. It's probably a little of both."

She sighed. "Oh, that makes me feel terrible."

"Then I'm sorry the subject came up." He became aware of a clatter outside in the hall, and before he could say anything more, a male aide came into the room with Rachel's dinner tray. He squeezed her hand. "And now I really have to go and let you eat your dinner."

"I'm not very hungry," she said, wrinkling her nose at the tray.

John shook his head. "Hungry or not, you have

to eat. Remember what you said about having to get stronger. Well, that's the way to do it."

"I guess you're right," she consented, good-humoredly.

"I know I am. Take care, Rachel, and I'll call you tomorrow."

"Good-bye," she said, and turned her attention to the dinner tray.

John wasn't very hungry either, but he knew he should take his own advice as well as give it. He considered going to the hospital cafeteria and eating there, but dismissed that idea quickly. Leaving the hospital he drove back downtown to the Hearthside Inn.

The restaurant was busy, but the hostess found a table for him set for two. She handed him a menu and removed the other place setting, then left him to decide what he wanted to eat.

In another few minutes a waiter came over, and John ordered the fillet of sole amandine. "And a tossed green salad with the house dressing," he said. "And coffee later."

While he waited for his meal to arrive he looked around to see if he might see somebody he knew. But all the couples around him—and they were all couples, no singles like himself—were unfamiliar to him. Unfamiliar and apparently blissfully happy —laughing and chatting, exchanging fond looks. It all depressed John, underscoring his loneliness.

When his sole arrived he was grateful to have something with which to occupy himself.

He finished his meal and coffee, and paid his

bill. Once in the car, he realized he couldn't remember what the fish had tasted like—or the salad either, for that matter.

He didn't know when he had felt so down. Pulling up at a traffic light, he shook his head, chastising himself for being so full of self-pity. Still he couldn't shake the feeling, and when the light turned green, he headed the car for home, if home was what he could call the furnished apartment he'd been living in since he'd left Pat.

The route to his apartment took him past his office and, stopping near there for another traffic light, he looked up to see the office lights still on. Surprised, he wondered if Barbara could still be up there working on the courthouse brief. But, no, he had the brief with him.

The light turned green, and he told himself he should continue on his way if only to get to the brief, but curiosity—and something else he couldn't define—forced him to pull over to the curb and park the car.

He unlocked the office door and went inside, calling out Barbara's name as he did so, not wanting to frighten her.

She was there.

"I can't believe you're still here," he said. "What are you working on?"

"Oh, nothing," she said, looking flustered. "Just some private correspondence. It's easier to do it here on the typewriter."

He cocked his head at her. "By private correspondence do you mean you've had another offer?"

Her cheeks flamed. "Yes."

John knew she had had two or three offers in the last few months from various law firms looking to bolster their ranks of female employees. He folded his arms. "I hope you're telling them no."

"Yes."

"Good." He walked with her back into her own office.

"Have you had a chance to look at the courthouse brief yet?" she asked him.

"No. I haven't been home yet. I went to the hospital to see Rachel, and then had dinner. I was on my way home just now when I saw the lights on up here." He waved to her typewriter with its half-written letter in the works. "Don't let me get in your way."

She walked around the desk and sat down at the typewriter while he sat in the chair on the other side. Barbara looked from the letter to him, then in a burst of speed finished typing the letter. She pulled it from the platen, turning off the typewriter as she did so.

"There," she said. "That's done." She turned to face him, her cheeks flaming again, and he became aware that he'd been staring at her. "Why are you looking at me like that?" she asked softly.

He felt his own face get hot. Unable to explain why, he searched for an answer. "I was admiring your dress," he said.

She looked down at herself. She was wearing a bright blue woolen dress, its bodice decorated with hand-sewn pearls and smocking, the puffy sleeves worn just below the elbow. She raised her gaze to him in disbelief. "But I've had it on all day."

"I know you have," he said hoarsely. "I admired it earlier. I just didn't say so."

"Oh," she said and lapsed into silence.

The silence grew and turned uncomfortable. John was about to take his leave when Barbara said, "How is Rachel?"

He supposed Barbara was more interested in bridging a conversational gap than in hearing how Rachel was. As far as he knew, they weren't acquainted with one another. But he recounted his visit to the hospital and going out to eat afterward at the Hearthside Inn. "It was crowded," he said.

"I've found it usually is," she answered. "I hate going there alone."

"I know what you mean. Well, next time I'm in need of a dinner companion, maybe you'll go there with me."

She smiled. She really had an exceptional smile, he noted. "I expect I could be persuaded."

Once again they lapsed into silence.

This time John got to his feet. "I might as well go on home and get into that courthouse brief. If I don't," he added, trying for a light touch, "you'll give me no peace in the morning."

"That's right," she said, picking up on the joke and laughing. She put the plastic cover over her typewriter. "I'll go out with you. As a matter of fact, I'm glad you're here to go out with. This building is a little on the dark and lonely side this time of night."

"Then, I'm glad I stopped," he said. "Here. Let me help you." He held up her raincoat for her to put it on.

"Thanks," she said, slipping into it.

Together they turned off the lights and left the office. As John locked the office door he thought how right Barbara was about the building being dark and lonely and turned to say as much to her—and found her this time staring at him. Even in the shadowy corridor he could see her cheeks redden. Not knowing what he intended, not intending anything really, he put his hand out to touch her face, and the next thing he knew she was in his arms and he was kissing her, gathering her more tightly to him, his kiss and her response becoming more and more ardent.

At last she pulled away and backed a space away from him. The conviction flooded through him that she was going to say she was sorry, and to his utter astonishment he felt tears sting his eyelids.

To his greater astonishment she said, "Maybe—I mean—would you like to come home with me, John?"

Now pleasure flooded through him. And desire. "I can't think of anything I'd like better."

She took his hand and he pulled her to him, and arm in arm they set off together down the hall, out of the building and to her apartment, where desire would become fulfillment.

Chapter Three
Second Thoughts

Sometimes, on her way to the office in the morning, Barbara would stop off at the florist's in the lobby and buy herself a flower for the bud vase on her desk. It gave her something pretty and refreshing to look at, especially when she was working on a brief that entailed a lot of research into dusty old law books. She usually bought a daisy, as they were inexpensive, long-lasting and, now that they came in so many different colors, offered the further advantage of variety.

The morning after she and John Randolph had made love together she stopped at the florist's, but this time—however foolish she felt doing it—she bought herself a pink rose. She would probably feel more foolish if John came into her office and saw the rose, but she would have to take that risk. The previous night had been special. The memory of it demanded a special flower, something she would be gazing at many, many times today. Gazing at and remembering.

John's secretary/receptionist, Gloria, was at her desk when Barbara walked into the office, and her pencil-thin eyebrows shot up. "Well!" she exclaimed. "What are we celebrating?"

Barbara's heart sank. She'd forgotten all about Gloria, who could probably see in her face what she was celebrating. Trying to look composed, Barbara said, "We're celebrating the completion of the courthouse brief."

Proof that her coverup had been successful was immediate. The anticipation on Gloria's heavily made-up face changed to disappointment. "Oh, that," she said with a dismissive wave of her bangled arm. "I thought at the very least you had a new boyfriend."

"Sorry, Gloria," Barbara said, and went into her office, where she sighed with relief and put the pink rose in the bud vase, getting water for it from the ladies' room.

Arranging it on her desk, she thought again about the previous night—for what seemed to be the sixteen hundredth time. She had meant it when she told John he was handsome. He was tall, with an athlete's build, but with a poet's face —sensitive, caring, with soft brown eyes and a full, sensuous mouth. And a wonderful shock of dark brown hair she'd run her hands through again and again.

She shivered. She had hoped John would spend the night with her, but he hadn't. Of course he hadn't come prepared to spend the night with her. It had been an impulsive, spur-of-the-moment invitation on her part, and the same kind of acceptance on his. Maybe next time he would spend the night.

She sat down at her desk and rested her chin on her hands. Surely there would be a next time. He had seemed as happy and excited—and as satisfied —last night as she had been.

Of course he was still married to Pat. But he had said yesterday it was a non-marriage, so he surely wouldn't stay married to her. And after that . . .

Barbara shivered again and hugged herself. She couldn't let herself think about that. It was much too soon—and too full of peril.

When John arrived at the office, Gloria had a number of pink telephone slips for him. Taking them from her, glancing at them, he stuffed them in his jacket pocket and took the courthouse brief out of his case, intending to hand it to her. "Will you give this to Barbara, please, when she comes in?"

"She's already here," Gloria said. "She's in her office."

He stood there holding the brief, undecided what to do. He wasn't exactly trying to avoid Barbara. He could hardly do that and go on working with her. But he wasn't up to seeing her right now, either. He held the brief out to Gloria. "Well, take it in to her, will you, please? Tell her that I've made some notes in the margins. I want to get on these phone calls."

"Sure," Gloria said, taking the brief.

John went on into his own office intent on returning the phone calls and beginning the day's work, but he couldn't get Barbara off his mind.

He wasn't at all sure he should have done what he did last night. He didn't know what Barbara was thinking or feeling. Maybe she was also having second thoughts. If she was, then there wouldn't be any problem. If she wasn't, if she was hoping for a repeat performance, well, then he didn't know what he was going to do. Maybe just plain level with her. Say he was sorry, he'd lost his head. Do better than that. Assume all the responsibility himself. Say he hadn't meant to lead her on, take advantage of her; he hoped she could forgive him.

Of course it had been very pleasant. More than pleasant. Fantastic. She had a voluptuous body, and once her shyness was overcome, she was a passionate lovemaker. Incredibly so.

John shook his head at himself, started to pick up the phone to get on with the return calls—and found himself looking at Pat.

It was only her picture with the family, of course, but it might as well have been Pat in person. He could have sworn she was gazing out at him with a look that said she was aware of his transgression against her, and how could he have done such a thing?

Irritated, feeling guilty as well, he picked up the picture and started to stuff it away in the bottom drawer of his desk. Then he stopped.

What would Gloria say when she came into his office and noticed the picture was missing? She wouldn't have the nerve to say anything to him, but she'd have plenty to say to the other secretaries in the building, and the first thing he knew, the story would be all over town about how his marriage was all washed up. And if anybody was going to start that story, it would be himself.

He returned the picture to its accustomed place, but still found himself unable to look at it. He got up from his desk and turned his back on the picture, stomping to the window to look out at another rainy day.

He was still standing there some minutes later, his work unattended, thoughts roiling through his head, when his buzzer sounded.

He picked up the phone. "Yes?" he snapped into it.

"Well, excuse me for living," Gloria said.

John swallowed. Gloria wore too much makeup and too few clothes, but she was far and away the best secretary he'd ever had. And his digression of the previous night had not been her doing. "I'm sorry," he said. "What can I do for you?"

"There's a Ms. DeWitt here to see you."

He frowned. "Who?"

"Ms. DeWitt. Ms. Tracey DeWitt."

"I've never heard of her."

"Shall I tell her that?"

Gloria was also too fresh, but he didn't say so and only hoped Ms. Tracey DeWitt, whoever she was, was not overhearing Gloria's end of this conversation. "No," he said. "Spare me that. And tell me this: does she have an appointment to see me?" Gloria sometimes made appointments for him without telling him she'd done so.

"No."

John glanced at his appointments pad. He had no idea who this woman was or why she wanted to see him, but he knew from past experience that off-the-street would-be clients seldom obliged him by leaving quietly. "All right," he said. "Show her in."

One glance at her confirmed the fact that he had never met her. He wouldn't have ever forgotten her. She was tall—almost as tall as he was—with a professional model's slender figure. And she was stunning to look at, her face thin with high cheekbones and flashing dark eyes and a mane of rich-colored hair.

And she knew she was stunning. She reveled in it.

Stretching a hand across his desk, he shook hands with her, noting she had a nice firm grip, and nodded to the client's chair. "Sit down, please."

She smiled, showing a flash of perfectly straight white teeth, and sat down. She was wearing a nubby white skirt and a turtleneck top to match it. Winter white, Pat would call it, though he had never understood the term. White was white, wasn't it? When she sat the slim skirt drew up over her knees, revealing slim legs, even slimmer ankles. Altogether she was something.

But he still didn't know why she wanted to see him. "May I ask, Ms. DeWitt, who recommended me to you?"

"A number of people, Mr. Randolph." A faintly

quizzical look replaced her smile. "Do you know Iris Delaney?"

"Yes. Not well, but I know her, yes."

"Well, I'm a friend of hers. At least I was a friend of hers." The smile again. "But if you know anything at all about Iris you know she can be, to put it politely, difficult."

"Yes. I know."

Tracey drew her hand across her throat. "And right now I've had it up to here with her." She glanced at her watch. "I'm catching an eleven-o'clock flight back to Washington, D.C. That's where I live. But I wanted to see you first."

He nodded neutrally, waiting for her to get to the point.

In addition to the nubby white wool outfit she was wearing, an oversize white leather handbag was slung over one shoulder. She pulled it into her lap, reached into it, and drew out an unsealed business-size envelope, which she tossed onto his desk. "I wanted to leave this with you."

He eyed the envelope but made no move to pick it up. "And what exactly," he said, "is this?"

"Some information," she answered, "concerning Iris and certain other people." She tossed the mane of raven hair. "Some vital information, I might add."

"I see," he said, though he didn't see at all. "But where do I come into it?"

She returned the handbag to her shoulder. "I asked around for the name of a lawyer I could give an important document to . . . trust him with."

She smiled that flashy smile again. "And you might be pleased to hear that your name led all the rest."

He tried an answering smile. "It's a nice compliment, certainly, and I accept it. But unfortunately I can't accept the document."

A shrewd look came into the dark eyes, and once again she pulled the oversize handbag into her lap. "You mean no fee, no service, right?" She pulled a billfold out of the handbag. "How much, Mr. Randolph?"

John shook his head. "You misunderstand. It's not the money, though there would of course be a small service charge. The point I was trying to make is that I can't accept any document from anybody sight unseen. I have to know what it is I'm entrusted with."

She shrugged her thin shoulders. "Then we don't have a problem. You can read what I've written. Here." She picked up the envelope and handed it to him. "Read it now if you want to."

He took the envelope from her. It contained a single sheet of paper. Headed "To Whom It May Concern," it consisted of two paragraphs written in a big, splashy handwriting. The first paragraph stated that on such-and-such a night Rachel Cory telephoned Iris Delaney looking for Mac Cory.

John frowned from the paper to Tracey. "I don't understand," he said. "The first paragraph, I mean, about Rachel calling Iris."

"That's the night she had her miscarriage," Tracey said. "She called Iris wanting to speak to Mac, saying it was important. Iris said her father couldn't be disturbed and hung up. Then afterward, when Iris realized that if she had let Rachel talk to Mac the miscarriage might have been prevented, and Rachel started raving in her delirium about calling Iris to speak to Mac, Iris claimed Rachel only dreamed she called her. And she's still claiming that. She even has Rachel believing it." Tracey spread her hands. "Now do you see?"

"Yes. Yes, I see." And indeed he did. He wondered if that was why Iris had been to see Rachel at the hospital. No wonder Rachel had looked so beaten down.

Putting that thought aside for the moment, he returned his attention to the paper, looking now at the second paragraph. It was just as damaging to Iris, stating that when she had married Robert, she had known full well he was the father of Clarice Hobson's baby, and she had married him before he could find that out for himself.

Again John looked from the paper to its author. "I gather what you're implying in this second paragraph is that if Robert had known he was the baby's father he would have married Clarice, not Iris."

"Correct."

John refolded the paper and slipped it back inside the envelope. "But there's still one thing I don't understand." He held up the envelope. "You say you want to entrust this information with me."

She nodded.

"Entrust it with me how?" he asked, frowning. "What am I supposed to do with it?"

"Oh, that," she said with a wave of her hand, her expression blithe, her tone of voice the same. "You can do whatever you want to with it. Sit on it. Go to the injured parties. Call a press conference. Whatever. I don't care. All I wanted was to have it off my mind—and off my conscience. And now it is." She gave him a bright smile. "And, for that small service charge you mentioned, it's now on your mind and your conscience." She stood up. "I must say I prefer it that way." Rummaging in the handbag she pulled out a card and handed it to him. "Send me a bill. Good-bye, Mr. Randolph."

She walked out, leaving John staring after her.

For the next few minutes he stood behind his desk staring at the envelope, feeling like a mischief maker, her words ringing in his mind: *Do whatever you want to with it. Sit on it. Go to the injured parties. Call a press conference. Whatever.*

At length he picked up the envelope and locked it inside the drawer of his desk, where he kept other confidential papers. He would have to sleep on the information and then decide what to do.

It seemed to Barbara that John was avoiding her. She told herself not to become neurotic. Many a day passed in the office when she scarcely laid eyes on him. He had a busy practice, and he was often in court, not to mention the many occasions when he might be available for conferring with her, while it was she who was tied up with something or somebody else.

Still, as the morning wore on toward noon, and

he made no attempt to seek her out, the feeling not only persisted, it grew.

It had started with Gloria bringing her the courthouse brief.

"Mr. Randolph asked me to bring you this," she said, handing it to her. "He said to tell you he made some notes in the margins here and there." She looked down at the pink rose in the bud vase. "I guess your celebration was a little premature."

Barbara couldn't think at first what she was talking about, and the uncertainty must have shown on her face.

"You know," Gloria added helpfully. "The pink rose."

"Oh, yes," Barbara said, remembering. She felt her face go hot and was sure Gloria would now know she had lied about the reason for the rose. She sought to keep her off the track by saying, "It was a silly thing to do, wasn't it? Buying myself a rose for that kind of reason?"

"I don't know. It's as good a reason as any, I guess. Well, I've got to get back outside. See you later." With a wave of her braceleted arm she was gone.

Barbara looked through the brief to see what notes John had made on it, disappointed he'd made any. She had thought she'd done a pretty thorough job. But she had wanted his input, so why be disappointed since that was exactly what he'd given her?

She put aside the appellate brief she had started working on and concentrated on revising the courthouse brief in light of John's notes, brightening at the prospect of having to take the brief into his office to say she couldn't make out his writing, or what did he mean by this remark, or did he have any idea where she could look up this notation?

But his handwriting was legible, his meaning in every instance was perfectly clear, and none of the notes called for her looking up anything. She sighed. The only excuse she was going to have for seeking him out was to take him the revised brief.

Inserting a fresh sheet of paper into her typewriter, she switched it on and tackled the first note.

She wondered when he had read the brief—after leaving her the previous night or getting up early that morning to do it?

She pictured him sitting at the breakfast table reading it that morning, dressing him in pale blue cotton pajamas and a thick blue terry-cloth robe, a cup of coffee at his elbow. Instant coffee probably. He wouldn't take the trouble or maybe have the right equipment for brewing coffee.

The next time he came to her apartment to make love to her, she would persuade him to stay the night, and then the next morning she would serve him a breakfast fit for a king. She sighed in anticipation. She could conjure up a whole series of mornings with a whole series of homemade breakfasts, each a little different from the one before.

And wouldn't he long to enter into a permanent relationship then? Marry her and make those wonderful breakfasts an everyday affair? And not just breakfasts, but dinners, too. And not just the domestic side of life either. A loving wife working

46

at his side during the day, sharing his evenings and his nights, there to confide in when he needed a listener, there to make love to when he desired her.

She was so full of thoughts of him she almost picked up her phone to call him, if only to say good morning.

And why not do it? she asked herself. Why wouldn't that be a perfectly acceptable thing to do? She could almost see the smile light up his face at the sound of her voice.

She picked up the receiver, then replaced it. If he was that eager to hear the sound of her voice, why hadn't he brought her the brief himself?

Or if he hadn't been able to bring it to her himself because he had a phone call waiting or something, why couldn't he have taken the call or whatever it was and then stuck his head in the door of her office to say good morning and how was she and whatever else he wanted to say.

Barbara glanced at her watch. More than half an hour had passed since Gloria had brought her the brief. And John had no pressing appointments that morning that she knew of. So why hadn't he come back to say hello?

Was it possible he was avoiding her? Was he already having second thoughts, already sorry he had accepted her invitation?

A deeper fear stabbed at her. Was it possible he had only said yes because he didn't want to hurt her feelings, because he didn't want to let her appear to be a fool for throwing herself at him the way she had?

She sat and stared at the little pink rose, almost unable to bear the sight of it and what it stood for.

Then she told herself that now was when she was being a fool. She had no reason to think all these stupid and hurtful things other than her own insecurity. For all she knew, John had been on the phone ever since stepping foot in his own office, immersed in some knotty legal problem, unable to get off the phone long enough to come back to say hello to her. And as soon as he could, he would make it up to her.

That didn't entirely satisfy her, but with an effort she turned her mind back to the revisions she had to make in the courthouse brief, and soon she was as immersed in that as she assumed John was in his knotty legal problem.

By the time she finished her revisions it was almost noon. She was pleased with the end result. John's notes had contributed solidly to the brief. She still had a lot to learn about the ins and outs of the law, and she was learning it from a master.

Her impulse was to take the revision straight to John. If he was in fact avoiding her, she'd be able to tell from his reaction. John was sensitive, but he wasn't subtle.

Looking in her pocket mirror to check her hair and her makeup, she picked up the papers and headed for John's office.

He was working at his desk. His door was open, but she didn't want to go barging in. She had done that yesterday, but things were different between them now. She tapped on the glass of the open door.

He looked up and, at sight of her, stood up smiling. "Well, good morning."

"Good morning," she said.

His smile was self-conscious, but then hers probably was, too. "I have the revisions," she said. "On the courthouse brief."

"Good." He held out his hand for them, and she went inside his office.

She wanted to close the door after her, but she was fearful of what Gloria might make of that. She and John never worked together with the door closed unless they were meeting together with a client. "Your notes were very helpful."

"I meant them to be," he said, waving to an empty chair. "Sit down while I go through this. If," he amended, "you have the time."

"Yes, I do," she said, sitting down.

He was almost to the last page of the revised brief when his intercom buzzer sounded. He picked up his phone, listened for a moment, then said, "Fine." Cradling the phone, he said, "Gloria's going to lunch."

"Oh," Barbara said, and couldn't think of anything to add to that.

He went back to the brief, and Barbara listened to the sounds of Gloria leaving the office, of the outer door closing, and then of silence settling in. Settling in and stretching out. She tried not to shift in the chair.

He finished the brief and handed it back to her. "It's fine," he said.

"You're sure?" she said, taking it.

He nodded. "Yes. You've done a good job with it. More than a good job. An excellent job."

She felt the color rising in her face. "With your help, John," she said.

He shrugged. "Most of the work was yours."

She didn't know what to say to that. She couldn't think of anything to say at all, in which case she had no excuse for staying. And he wasn't inviting her to.

Disappointment flooded through her. He had been avoiding her after all. He was having second thoughts.

"Well, I might as well get back to work." She stood up and he made no move to stop her. In fact, he seemed to be relieved to have her go.

She started out of his office. "I'm sorry, Barbara," he said, his words stopping her. "I meant to speak to you before about this." He was holding out a pink telephone slip to her. "Gloria gave this to me when I came in this morning, but the name doesn't ring any bells with me. Maybe it's something you're involved in?"

He came around the desk to show it to her. "Yes. It's for me." She reached to take it.

Their hands brushed together, setting hers tingling. His too, apparently. Before she could take a breath he had her in his arms and he was kissing her, his mouth pressed urgently against hers, pulling her tightly to him.

For a few breathless moments she gave herself to the kiss, desire for him flooding through her. Her earlier decision, made only moments ago, to hold herself away from him dissolved into nothingness. But then she pulled away from him. "No, John, we can't. We mustn't."

He sighed. "I know. You're right. Forgive me."

She wasn't sure what she was to forgive him for, but one thing was certain. She wasn't going to spend another morning like the one she'd just now gotten through. She had to know exactly how he felt, what his position was.

"I only meant," she said, "that we can't behave like this here in the office. I shudder to think what would happen if Gloria suddenly came back from lunch."

"Yes," he said. "I know exactly what you mean." He moved a few steps away from her.

"But," she went on, "I didn't mean anything other than that." She searched his face, trying to read from his expression if he agreed with her.

He seemed to. He moved toward her again, one hand out to her.

She swallowed for courage. "Maybe you'd like to come home again with me tonight?"

He hesitated only a moment, glancing at something on his desk, then turning his back on it resolutely. "Yes, my darling. I'd like that very much."

She could have floated back to her office on the strength of that "darling" alone, but he gave her more reason to float. Closing the door of his office, he took her in his arms once more, kissing and caressing her until she thought she might faint with desire for him.

She had to pull away from him again, and this time she left his office before anything more could start up between them.

She was still breathless when she reached her own office, and she closed the door after her. It was far too soon for the absent Gloria to return, but she was taking no chances.

She didn't even try to return to work. It would have been pointless. She was far too stirred up. She would simply sit at her desk until she could calm herself, and then she'd go out for lunch herself.

And while she was out she would go to that wonderful new gourmet food shop and buy something elegant for dinner. She hadn't said anything to John about his having dinner with her, but she was sure he would. And what fun it would be to actually cook for him, not just dream about it.

And she would pick up some breakfast rolls, too. She also hadn't said anything to John about spending the night, but with this much advance knowledge surely he would, even if it meant driving to his apartment during his own lunch hour to pick up his shaving things and toothbrush and whatever.

With a shiver of delight Barbara took a small memo pad and began making a list of the food she wanted to buy. In her state of excitement she couldn't trust herself to rely on memory alone.

She had finished her list and made some mental notes about what table linens and china and glassware she would use tonight—and oh, yes, she must buy some candles, too—and was on her way to the ladies' room before going out when her buzzer sounded.

Realizing Gloria must be back from lunch, she crossed to the phone and picked it up.

"You have a phone call," Gloria said, "from Mrs. Randolph."

Both surprised and bewildered, Barbara said, "You mean Pat?"

"Yes. Will you take the call?"

"Well, yes, of course. Put her on."

Gloria clicked off, and Pat Randolph clicked on. "Barbara?" she said.

"Yes, Pat. How are you?"

There was a sigh at the other end of the line. "Only so-so." Quickly she amended that. "I don't mean physically. Physically I'm fine. It's just that —well, the reason I'm calling you is I have to talk to you."

Barbara's bewilderment increased. She couldn't imagine what in the world she wanted to talk to her about. "Well, all right. But what about?"

"About John. I—I need your help. Will you help me?"

Barbara swallowed, her mind racing. "Well, of course. If I can." She couldn't imagine what kind of help she could give Pat where John was concerned—or what kind of help Pat wanted. Was it possible she wanted legal help from her, maybe wanted her to represent her in her divorce from John?

That would be a bit sticky, wouldn't it, especially in view of her own budding romance with him? But Pat couldn't know anything about that. "What kind of help do you want from me, Pat?" she finally prompted.

There was another sigh. "I want him back, Barbara, and I need your help in doing that."

Chapter Four
To Tell or Not to Tell

In the silence that followed Pat's bombshell statement, Barbara tried desperately to think what to say. "Pat, I'm not sure I—what I mean is—" She swallowed and started over. "What I'm trying to say is I don't know what help I can give you—if I'm the person you really want."

Pat sighed again. "You're the only person I've got."

Barbara didn't see how that could be. Pat had a sister and a brother and a father, not to mention her two grown children. But she probably didn't want to involve her children, and maybe the rest of her family couldn't be of any help, either. She swallowed again. "Of course I'll help you if I can. Only I don't see—"

Pat cut in. "Could you meet with me, Barbara, and let me talk to you and explain how I think you can help?"

"Well, when would you suggest?"

"You're the one who has a schedule to keep," Pat said. "My time is pretty free. You say when."

Barbara wished she had left the office before this call came in, but she supposed there would have been a pink telephone slip waiting on her return. "I was just going out to lunch when you called, Pat. Do you want to meet me somewhere, or is this too short notice?"

"No, I can meet you."

"All right. How about that new place called the Salad Bar?"

"That would be fine."

"Say in ten minutes."

"I'll be there."

The call completed, Barbara cradled the receiver. Then she opened her handbag, took out the list she had made for that night, wadded it up, and dropped it in the wastebasket on her way out of the office.

John was working at his desk when Barbara tapped on the glass of his open door. He gave her a pleased look. "Come in. Did you have a nice lunch?"

"I've had better."

He frowned. "Is something the matter?"

"Not exactly, no. But I have to take back my offer about tonight. I already had an engagement. I'd forgotten about it."

"Oh. We'll do it another time, then. Are you sure you're all right?"

"Yes, I'm fine. Well—I'll get back to work, then."

He nodded. "Okay. And we'll talk later."

She turned and left, and for a minute or two he sat there looking at the doorway where she had been. Admit it or not, something had upset her. Maybe her prior commitment was a date with another man, and she had tried unsuccessfully to get out of it.

Shrugging, John returned to the notes he was making for an upcoming case. To tell the truth he was a bit relieved that Barbara couldn't keep their date tonight. Despite the magnetism she held for him—and it was a powerful, sometimes over-whelming one—he still wasn't sure he wanted to get involved with her. And while one coming together hardly constituted an involvement, a return engagement probably would.

Satisfied that everything was working out for the best, John returned to the case he was working on but found it hard to concentrate, found the after-noon passing with an almost unbearable slowness.

He forced himself to continue working until six, then drove out to his country club for a non-alcoholic drink in the bar. Finding nobody to attach himself to, he drove back into town, stopped at a deli for a take-out sandwich and soda, and drove home to his apartment. He told himself that if he was going to stay estranged from Pat, he would have to find himself a more pleasant place to live, a place he could look forward to coming home to.

He spent a restless evening and a restless night, and he went back to the office the next morning in a grumpy mood. On his desk was the statement Gloria had typed up to send to Tracey DeWitt for taking and keeping the document she had brought to him.

He'd forgotten about it until this reminder, and he didn't like having to think about it now. Opening the locked desk drawer he took the envelope out and reread the statement.

His troubles with Steve Frame had started with the issue of blackmail, and that was what this document smacked of. He wished he'd never agreed to keep it, though once in possession of the information, it hardly mattered whether or not he had the document.

He put out a hand toward the phone to call Rachel, then changed his mind. He would wait until she was home from the hospital and better able to deal with the information.

Replacing the document in the drawer, he turned his attention to the case he'd been working on the afternoon before, and told himself what he'd told himself many, many times before: work was the answer to personal problems. Immerse himself in his work, and put everything else aside. The result was a productive morning, and that put him in a better mood—until Gloria buzzed him just before lunch to remind him that he and Barbara were having lunch with Mr. Watkins, a client of theirs.

He'd forgotten about that, too.

Watkins had set up the lunch date, ostensibly to talk about his appeal, but it became clear to John over the onion soup—and clearer still over the cheese soufflé that followed—that Watkins was basically there to make time with Barbara.

Nor was she doing anything to discourage him.

By the time coffee was served John could scarcely contain his irritation, and when at long last he and Barbara saw Watkins into a cab, then started back to the office on foot, he had all he could do not to blow up at her.

Walking alongside him, she sighed. "I'll be glad when this case is over and done with. What a tiresome man he is."

John turned to her in astonishment. "Tiresome? All through lunch you acted as if you could hardly get enough of him."

"I was only trying to be polite. He is a client, after all."

"Yes," John agreed, "he certainly is—for your affections."

Barbara waved a dismissive hand. "You exaggerate. He's a lonely, embittered man with nothing better to do than take a neighbor to court for tearing down some mangy old hedges he swears were on his property."

John grunted. Barbara was simply handing back to him—in somewhat different words—an appraisal of Watkins that he himself had made a few weeks earlier, but he wouldn't give her the satisfaction of admitting that.

Nor would he give her the further satisfaction of seeing how unsettled she had made him feel. He changed the subject to the "courthouse business," letting it occupy them the rest of the way back to the office.

But his attempts to immerse himself in his work were not so successful that afternoon, and finally he pushed back from his desk, crossed from his office into hers, closed the door behind him, and asked to see the revised courthouse brief.

She got up to get it for him, and when she handed it to him he pulled her into his arms and kissed her with all the pent-up passion the day had built in him.

At first she didn't respond, indeed tried to pull away from him, but after a few moments she gave in to him, matching urgency with urgency.

A few moments later she wrenched free of him, saying, "John, please. We mustn't."

"I have to," he said, and tried to pull her to him once again.

But this time she fended him off, and at the same time her buzzer sounded. Gloria had a phone call for her.

Disappointed, further frustrated, and as irritated at himself now as he had been earlier at her, he returned to his own office, barely remembering to take the courthouse brief with him.

He sought her out again at the end of the day, asking her to have dinner with him, confident that after dinner was over she would take him home with her, but she turned down his invitation, claiming she had another engagement.

And so it went for the rest of the week. All he managed to get from her was a couple of passionate embraces, followed by her pulling away from him, saying they mustn't.

After a lonely, desperation-filled weekend, John went into the office Monday morning determined to have a showdown with Barbara. Dispatching Gloria to the courthouse with some papers to be filed there, he walked into Barbara's office and once again closed the door behind him.

Glancing up she said, "Gloria is going to start wondering what's going on."

He shook his head. "Gloria is on her way to the courthouse to do some errands for me." He held out his hands. "Come here. Please."

"No," Barbara said, staying behind her desk.

He stretched his hands out farther. "If you only knew how I feel."

Barbara, luscious in pink and white, gave him a wry look. "If you only knew how *I* feel."

"Show me."

"No, John."

"Darling." He didn't mind pleading. He would do anything to have her. "Darling," he said again.

She shook her beautiful blond head. "No."

He couldn't understand it. She had resisted him before, but never for as long as this, and never without first giving in to him a little. He started to plead with her again, then changed tactics. He knew what she wanted to hear, what he supposed all women wanted to hear. Well, it wouldn't be much of a lie. "Darling," he said a third time, "I love you. You must know that."

That did it, as he had known it would. She got up from her desk and came around to stand before him. "Oh, John, do you mean that?"

"Of course I do."

He put his arms around her and drew her to him, and this time she did not resist him, responding to his kiss with an intensity that matched his own.

A few moments later, however, she pulled away from him again, saying, "John, we just can't."

"All right," he said. "I know. Not here."

"Not here or anywhere. Not the way things are. Oh, John," she continued, turning a beseeching face to him, "I love you too, but we can't go on acting like a couple of sneak thieves, hugging and kissing behind Pat's back."

"Pat has nothing to do with us."

"She has everything to do with us. You're still married to her." She held up a hand. "And don't tell me it's a non-marriage. In the eyes of the law it's a marriage."

He spoke without thinking. "Well, it won't be for long."

As he should have expected, Barbara jumped on that. "Do you mean you've spoken to Pat about a divorce?"

"No."

"Have you spoken to her at all?"

"No. Not yet."

She turned away from him. "Then there's your answer."

Taking hold of her wrist, he pulled her back to him. He tried to turn it into an embrace, but she wouldn't let him.

"No, John. Not until you settle things with Pat. I refuse to compete with her. You have to choose between us. Either it's Pat or it's me. It can't be both of us."

He had known it would come to this. "All right," he said, "I'll speak to Pat."

Barbara gave him an uncertain look. "And what will you say?"

"Whatever I have to to make her understand that she and I are finished. Will that satisfy you?"

To his surprise, Barbara gave him a quick little hug. "Oh, darling, yes. Yes, it will."

Before he could turn the embrace into anything more, she had retreated to the safety of the other side of her desk, leaving John no option but to return to his own office.

There he seated himself at his desk and picked up the phone to call Pat, but he found himself staring at his family's picture. Eventually he put the receiver back in its cradle, unable to make the call.

Mondays were normally among the busiest days. Each of his clients had had an entire weekend to brood about unmade support payments or custody disputes or property settlements or whatever. The phones were seldom still. And this particular Monday was no exception, so his failure to call Pat was not entirely a failure of will. It was at least partly the press of business.

In fact he was just hanging up from a long and largely fruitless conversation with a client when Barbara, still looking luscious in her pink and white sweater and skirt, poked her head in his office.

"May I come in?" she said.

He waved her to the chair. "Of course. What can I do for you?"

"I wanted to know if you've spoken to Pat."

He should have known. He took a breath and made a decision. "Yes, I spoke to her just a few minutes ago."

Barbara's eyes lighted up. "And is everything settled?"

"Darling," John said, "not on the phone. I couldn't do that to her."

The light flickered away. "No, I don't supoose you could. But you must have said something to her."

"Yes. I made an appointment with her."

Some of the light flickered back. "For when?"

He shook his head. "Not until later this week. That was as soon as she had any time."

A shadow of disbelief crossed Barbara's face, but then she shrugged and said, "Well, at least something is in the works."

"That's right. And now that it is, will you have dinner with me tonight?"

She stood up. "No, John. Making an appointment with Pat to speak to her about a divorce doesn't come under the heading of settling things with her. And we have to wait for that. At least I have to. I couldn't live with myself otherwise."

Before he could object or plead anew, she left his office.

It was just as well, he told himself, getting up from his desk to stand at the window and look out at the people on the sidewalk below. He was beginning not to know himself, and that made him uncomfortable. The reason those various people had recommended him to Tracey DeWitt was because of his long reputation as honest and trustworthy. Yet today he had told two lies to Barbara, who certainly deserved better than that.

He was more than uncomfortable. He was filled with self-loathing.

Turning from the window back to his desk he made up his mind to undo one lie at least. He would call Pat and make that appointment with her.

Resolutely he dialed her number. There was no answer.

About to slam down the phone, he broke the connection instead and dialed Rachel's number. He knew she was home from the hospital. He had run into Mac on the street a day ago.

Rachel's voice came on at the other end of the line.

"Rachel, it's John Randolph. How are you?"

"Oh, John, how nice to hear from you. I'm fine. Well, maybe not all the way fine yet, but practically there."

"Good. I'm glad to hear it. Rachel, I'm calling to ask you if you are acquainted with a woman named Tracey DeWitt."

"Yes. She's a friend of Iris's."

"Yes, I know that." He paused, uncertain how to proceed. Or if to proceed. Why add to Rachel's distress? Why not simply let well enough alone?

His hesitation lasted so long Rachel spoke up. "What about Tracey? I mean, why are you asking me about her?"

"Oh," he said lamely, "no reason really. Somebody mentioned her to me, asking me if I knew her, and I said I didn't. I just wondered if you did. Forget I mentioned it. I really called to see how you are."

Now the uncertainty was in her voice. "It's like I said before, I'm fine. Or practically so."

"Have you gotten your appetite back?"

"Yes."

"That's good. Are you taking care of yourself?"

"Yes."

"And Mac—how is he doing?"

"He's fine, too. He just came in from working in the garden most of the afternoon, mostly getting in the gardener's way."

John laughed. "Well, I'm glad to hear everything's okay. Maybe you'll have lunch with me soon, Rachel."

"Yes, I'd like that."

"I'll give you a call next week."

"Yes, John. Please do."

"All right, then. Good-bye." John broke the connection and dialed Pat's number once again. There was still no answer. He hung up the phone and went back to staring out the window, still unhappy with himself. Not only would Barbara call him a liar if she knew the truth about him, but Rachel must think he was crazy, as well.

Rachel didn't think John was crazy, but she was certainly puzzled by his phone call.

Turning to Mac, who was now settling on the living room sofa with the afternoon paper, she said, "I don't understand."

Without looking up, Mac patted the sofa cushion beside him. "What don't you understand?" he asked, as Rachel sat down next to him.

"Why John Randolph called me just now."

Mac put the paper down and turned to her. "From what I heard of your conversation, it sounded to me like he called to ask how you were."

She took one of Mac's hands in hers. "I know. And that's what he said."

"Well, then?"

"But when I first got on the phone he said he was calling to ask me if I was acquainted with Tracey DeWitt."

Mac took up his paper again. "Why did he want to know that?"

"I don't know. He didn't say. I have a feeling he was going to tell me something having to do with her but then changed his mind."

Mac turned from the front page to an inside one. "Does John know Tracey?"

"No. At least he said he didn't."

"I'd forget about it, then. It couldn't have been important."

She sighed. "No, I suppose not."

Mac's gaze left the paper and searched her face. "You surely aren't thinking that John would lie to you, are you?"

"He might. I lied to him."

Mac cocked his gray head at her. He had been gray when she first had met him, but she had never thought of him as old. He was so filled with vitality. It shone in his dark eyes, in the upward lift of his chin, in the firmness of his physique. And yet lately . . .

"I'm sorry, Mac," she said, aware he had put a question to her. "What did you ask me?"

"I said how did you lie to John? In saying you were fine, or practically so?"

She shook her head again. "No. I lied to him in saying you were fine."

Mac had been about to immerse himself again in his newspaper. Instead he put it down. "But I am fine," he said.

"No, you aren't." She reached out to touch his face with the tip of her finger. "Do you think I've been married to you all this time without knowing anything about you?"

"No," he said, shaking his head. "I don't think that."

"Then, don't tell me you're all right when you're not. Something is bothering you."

"If anything is bothering me, it has to do with the newspaper business, not you."

"No, it's something more important than that."

He got up from the sofa. "You're imagining things."

She stood up, too. "No, I'm not."

With a little wave of his hand he walked out of the room. Rachel would have followed him, but she decided with a sigh that it was fruitless. Something was eating away at Mac, but if he wouldn't tell her what it was, there was no way she could find out otherwise. And to continue to press him to tell her might irritate him to the point of snapping at her, and she didn't want that. The closeness of their relationship was too precious to her to want to jeopardize it with needless quarreling.

Maybe in time he would tell her.

Or maybe, with any luck, she could find out what it was some other way.

Chapter Five
Entreaties and Rebuffs

The following Saturday—a rainy, chilly day more like late winter than early spring—Pat drove to John's apartment. After finding a parking place she stayed on in the car for a while, uncertain of her mission, telling herself she should have called him first. For all she knew, he might have somebody up there in the apartment with him.

The mission had been Barbara's idea.

Pat thought back to their luncheon Monday at the Salad Bar. They had agreed to eat first and talk afterward, and though each of them had tried to introduce some neutral topic of conversation while they were making their way through their abundant salads, the efforts had trickled away into silence.

Constrained silence. More so, Pat thought, on Barbara's part than on her own.

"It's probably unfair of me," Pat had said to her when at last the table was cleared. "Putting this burden on you, I mean."

"No. Not at all," Barbara had answered.

"Though I'm not sure I can be any help to you. I mean," she added, her voice thick with constraint, "you know him so much better than I do."

"Yes," Pat agreed, "but sometimes a third person, somebody not involved in the situation, has a clearer judgment on how to resolve it."

Unaccountably Barbara flushed and looked somewhere across the room. Or had she looked across the room first and then flushed?

Sitting in the car thinking back on it, Pat couldn't be sure. Maybe Barbara had caught sight of somebody or something that embarrassed her. That would explain the flush. She put it out of her mind and thought back to the heart of their conversation.

"I think," Barbara said, "you ought to talk to him."

"Apologize to him, you mean?" Pat asked.

Barbara had taken her paper napkin up from the table and was tearing it to pieces, bit by bit. And she flushed again. "All right, yes. I guess that's what I was thinking and didn't have the nerve to say."

"Barbara," Pat put in quickly, realizing Barbara was probably uncomfortable getting involved in family affairs, "I want you to be frank. That's why I asked you to meet with me—instead of going to somebody in my family. Because I felt you'd be more objective."

Barbara's color deepened, but she put the napkin down. "All right. Then, I think you should apologize and explain to him. Try to get him to see your side of it. And Marianne's."

Unaccountably, just as unaccountably as Barbara's heightened color, Pat felt a stir of hope. John must have said something to Barbara. "And do you think that will do it for me? Do you?"

There was such pain in Barbara's eyes Pat could hardly bear to go on looking at her. "Oh, I can't say that. I—" She swallowed. "I don't have any idea."

Pat sank back in her chair. "I'm sorry. I didn't mean to put you on the spot. Of course you don't have any idea. Nobody does but John." Impulsively she reached across the table and squeezed Barbara's hand. "Thank you for your suggestion. And that's what I'll do—go see him to apologize and explain." She crossed her fingers. "Wish me luck."

The look Barbara gave her this time was unreadable, and when she spoke, her voice seemed to be thick with emotion. "Good luck, Pat."

Sitting in the car, trying to get her nerve up to do what she had said she would, Pat found herself wondering again about Barbara's constraint and what could have caused it. Maybe she hadn't wanted to meet with her and had only agreed because Pat had insisted on it. Barbara probably hated being put in the middle between her boss and his estranged wife.

After a few more minutes, Pat opened the door and got out. If she was going to do it, then do it. Sitting here brooding about it would not accomplish anything. And if John did have somebody up there in the apartment with him, well, he didn't have to answer the door, did he?

He answered the door. And nobody was there

with him. "Come in, Pat," he said, opening the door wider.

She looked around as she walked in. She had known the apartment he'd taken was a furnished one, but she hadn't been prepared for how depressing it would be. It looked like a motel room of the ancient past—drab green draperies at the windows, cheap maple furniture, a rug of uncertain color on the floor. How could John be happy here after the airy brightness and spaciousness of their home, with all its tasteful furnishings?

He cleared some papers from a shabby gray armchair and formally said, "Won't you sit down?"

She perched on the edge of it, trying to keep her face from displaying the distaste she had for the chair and the room in general. She didn't want to make him defensive.

He sat on the couch opposite her. "What can I do for you?"

"I'd like to apologize, John."

"You've already done that."

"Well, yes, I know, but—" She spread her hands in what she hoped was a conciliatory gesture. "I want to apologize again. I really didn't understand before how you felt. I think I do now."

He said nothing.

"And I wanted to explain. I mean, Marianne couldn't bear to have you know. You mean so much to her, John, and she was so ashamed—and terrified that you'd stop loving her."

John shook his head. "You should have known better than that."

"I did know better than that. But I couldn't persuade her of it, and when she swore me to secrecy, well, I—"

"You shouldn't have let her swear you to secrecy."

"I know I shouldn't have, but at the time . . ." Pat let her voice trail off. This wasn't going at all well, and she couldn't think of how to make it go better. In desperation she fell back on what she had told him at the time of their estrangement. "John, I was only trying to spare your feelings. It would have hit you hard, wouldn't it? Wouldn't it, John?"

"Yes," he admitted. "It would have."

"Well, then, at least you see why I did what I did, don't you?"

It was a few moments before he nodded and said, "Yes, I see why."

Was he softening? Did she dare let herself believe that he wanted to put their misunderstandings behind them and start anew as much as she did?

Impulsively Pat got up from the shabby gray armchair and went to sit beside him on the couch. "Darling," she said, putting a hand on his arm, "all I want—all I've ever wanted—is for you to be happy."

It was as though she had touched a raw nerve with a branding iron. He shot up from the couch, turning to glare down at her, his brown eyes flashing. "That's a lie! All you've ever wanted is what suits your own purposes. Starting from the day we were married."

She stared up at him in disbelief.

He turned away from her and stalked across the room. "I've had all I can take of it."

She was still staring at him, at his back now, in disbelief. "John," she entreated him, "please. You must listen to me. For the children's sake, if not for ours. Do you think it was easy for me to come here like this, uninvited and probably unwanted?" She nearly choked on the words. "Please, I beg you."

"All right," he said, not turning around. "I'm listening."

"You have to believe me. Keeping you in the dark about Marianne did not suit me or my purposes. I wanted to tell you."

He still would not turn to her. "It's easy to say that."

She felt anger begin to rise up in her. "Nothing is easy to say to you. You said you would listen to me, but I don't believe you are. It's like talking to a stone wall."

He spun around to her. "All right. Then you listen to me. I'm your husband, and as your husband I should have come first in your regard. Not Marianne, not Michael. Me."

"You do come first in my regard. You always have. I have told you over and over again that I was wrong to do what I did, that I made a mistake in judgment, that I was only trying to spare your feelings. How can you charge one mistake against all the years we've had together and come up on the debit side?"

"Because it isn't one mistake. There've been others."

Her anger flared. "Yes, there have been. I never said I was perfect. But there have also been mistakes on your side. Do those not count?"

He didn't answer her.

She made one last try. "John, we have always been able to forgive and forget. That's been one of the strengths of our marriage. Are you telling me now you can't forgive me for this latest mistake of mine?"

"That's right."

She gasped. "I don't believe you. You can't have changed that much these last few months."

"You can believe what you want to, Pat. But what it all comes down to is I can't rely on your love or your loyalty any longer. You talk one thing and do another. Cast me out, then ask me back in. Side with the children against me, then claim it was in my interest. And then you ask me to forgive you, sweep it all aside as though nothing at all ever happened"—he snapped his fingers—"and, presto, the little white rabbit disappears." He shook his head. "Well, I'm sorry, but I can no longer accommodate you."

Rubbing the side of her face as if he had slapped her, she stood up to leave. She had been a fool to come here. "There has to be more of a reason for your talking the way you have. I can only assume you've taken up with somebody else. Some other woman."

"Well, you're wrong. I haven't."

"I don't believe you. Something has happened to turn you into a stranger, to turn you into a person I no longer know. You talk about counting on somebody. I counted on you to open your heart and your mind to me. But somebody else has hold of your heart now."

He was back to glaring at her. "That's not true!"

"Isn't it?"

"No!"

She made a face. "You should look at yourself in the mirror, John. You look just like the little boy who gets caught with his hand in the cookie jar." A lock of her hair had fallen across her forehead. She pushed it back. "All right. I suppose you want me to see a lawyer."

"No."

She didn't understand him at all. "Are you saying you don't want a divorce?"

"That's right."

"And the other woman doesn't want you to get a divorce?"

"I've told you there's no other woman."

"I know what you told me, and I still don't believe you." She picked up her purse. "I'll find myself a lawyer and have him—or her—get in touch with you."

She started to leave, but he strode across the room to her, grabbing her wrist. "I told you I don't want a divorce."

Anger flared up in her again, and she twisted away from him. "You also told me you can't forgive me and you can't accommodate me—meaning you don't want to come back to me. But you insist there's no other woman and you don't want a divorce."

"That's right."

She shook her head. "You're not making any sense. But all right, John. You tell me. What do you want?"

He only looked at her, saying nothing.

"Well? You must want something."

For the space of a breath she thought he was going to burst into tears. Then the moment passed and he glowered at her. "I want to be left alone."

Furious now that she had let her own silly hopes put something in him that obviously wasn't there, she snapped at him, "Well, that's fine and dandy. And easy to do." Pushing him out of the way, she stormed out of his apartment, slamming the door behind her.

When she reached her car she was trembling all over with anger and humiliation and, yes, bewilderment. Whatever John said, whatever he didn't say, more was going on than met the eye.

She wondered for a moment if he could have something physically wrong with him, if that could explain the contradictions in him. Why should he want a nonfunctioning marriage? What possible advantage was there to him in that?

Pat opened the driver's door and got into the car. With a shake of her head, she put the key in the ignition and started the engine, then headed for home.

Marianne wasn't there when she arrived. Even before determining that fact, Pat could tell by the silence that hung in every room like a palpable thing. Marianne was probably still with Michael at his off-campus apartment.

With a sigh, Pat settled in the living room, seeing again in her mind's eye John's grim little apartment. Even on a rainy day like this one her living room was bright and beautiful. She idly rubbed a hand along the back of the yellow sofa. Beautiful, yes, but what a lonely one.

And so unnecessarily so. She had gone to John's apartment believing she could bridge the gap between them, soothe his wounded feelings, work out their differences.

Instead he had humiliated her, rebuffed her. And, she was almost certain, lied to her. There had to be another woman in his life. It had been written all over his face. Yet why would he lie? What was the point now?

The doorbell rang, startling her from her reverie.

Instinctively she glanced at her watch. Almost three in the afternoon. She wasn't expecting anybody. Was it possibly John?

Telling herself she was being a fool all over again she nevertheless hastened to the front door and opened it.

Liz Matthews stood on the doorstep.

"Oh," Pat said.

"Well, is that all I get by way of greeting?" Liz demanded.

With a sigh Pat opened the door wider. "Come in, Aunt Liz."

She came in, though "swept in" would have more aptly described it. Tall, imperious, her color-touched hair in an upsweep, her beige and black suit looking as if it had been made for her—and undoubtedly it had—Liz preceded Pat into the house and went on into the living room without waiting to be asked there. "I called you earlier," she said, "but you were out."

"Yes," Pat answered, adding nothing more. Aunt Liz was one of the worst gossips in Bay City, and Pat refused to say anything incriminating.

Liz ensconced herself where Pat had been sitting, naturally. She always managed to outmaneuver everybody in whatever she did, Pat thought.

"Well, what were you doing out?"

"Errands. Nothing of any importance."

Liz sniffed as if she didn't believe her.

She probably didn't, Pat decided, and decided further to engage in a bit of tit for tat. "What did you come to see me about, Aunt Liz?"

Liz drew herself up. "I didn't know I had to have a reason to come see you, Patricia."

"I didn't say you did, but you generally do have a reason for coming here."

"Well, all right, if you insist. I came to ask you about John."

Pat had suspected as much. She was sorrier by the minute that she had answered the doorbell's ring. Had she known it was Liz, she would have pretended not to be home. "What about him?"

"Have you made up with him?"

"No."

"Well, have you tried making up with him?"

"Aunt Liz, I don't really feel . . ."

She let the sentence trail off, but her aunt finished it for her. "You don't feel it's any of my business."

Pat squared her shoulders. "All right, yes. I don't."

"Then why did you make it my business?"

Pat frowned in renewed bewilderment. "How did I make it your business?"

"By making me feel I owed you an apology for thinking that Barbara Weaver had designs on your husband and that your husband was doing little, if anything, to discourage her."

"It was more than thinking, Aunt Liz."

"Very well. *Saying*, then. At least I have the decency to say what's on my mind."

Pat's temper began to flare again. "Is that what you call it? Decency?"

"Would you rather I'd whispered it around town?"

"I'd rather you'd kept your suspicions to yourself, especially since there was nothing to them."

"You don't expect me to believe that, do you?"

"I thought you said you felt as if you owed me an apology. This doesn't sound like much of an apology to me."

Liz brushed that aside. "You'll never convince me it was brains or ability John had in mind when he hired that woman."

"Barbara can't help it that she's pretty."

Liz arched one eyebrow. "Is that what you call it—pretty? With those measurements? I call it so overblown as to be vulgar."

Pat waved her hand in a gesture of dismissal. "Well, call it what you want to. I have better things to do with my time than sitting here talking about Barbara or her measurements."

"Or her involvement with John?" Liz asked, giving her a condescending look.

Pat clenched her fists. "Barbara is not involved with John. She wasn't a few months ago, and she isn't now."

"Then whom is he involved with?"

Without thinking Pat said, "He says he's not involved with anybody."

Immediately Liz pounced. "Then you have been talking to him."

Pat tried to keep the red out of her face, a battle that was lost before it was ever begun. "Yes, I've been talking to him. He is still my husband."

The condescending look again. "In a manner of speaking, yes, I suppose he is."

Pat was barely able to contain herself. "Aunt Liz, you came here talking about an apology—one that you still haven't made, I might add—and all you've done is poke and probe, insinuate and insult. And I'm supposed to sit here and take it all?"

Liz patted her hair. "I've only made a few observations, Patricia. Whether or not you act on them is your decision, one I certainly wouldn't make for you."

"Not much, you wouldn't," Pat muttered.

Liz frowned. "Speak up, dear. You mustn't let the failure of your marriage turn you into a dowdy mutterer. And, really, don't you think that dress has just about had it?"

Pat looked down at the pink velvet dress. Yes, it was a bit on the worn side. And trust her aunt not only to notice it, but make a point of mentioning it. "Aunt Liz," she said, trying her best not to explode, "I'm not in the mood to discuss my wardrobe. It's been a difficult day."

Liz smiled placatingly. "All those errands you spoke of. I don't suppose one of them involved a drive over to John's apartment, did it?"

That did it. Jumping to her feet, Pat glared at her aunt. "Stop it right now! If it means so much to you that you can't bear to live not knowing it, then yes, I went over to see John this afternoon, and no, it wasn't a very satisfactory conversation we had." She put up a warning hand. "And that is all I'm going to say about it. You can trick and badger me right into the grave, but you're not going to get one more word out of me. All right?"

Liz drew herself higher than before. "Really, my dear, I'm not the least bit interested in what transpired between you and John."

"Oh, no, of course you're not," Pat said, her voice heavy with sarcasm. "You're sitting there dying to know what we said and what we did or didn't do. Because you're nothing but a nosy old snoop, and as far as I'm concerned, I never want to see you again."

Liz's eyes were wide with shock. "Well, really," she said, standing up. "I knew you were upset, Patricia. But I didn't know you were capable of saying such terrible things to me. You'll forgive me if I don't stay to hear more. Don't bother to see me out. I'm quite capable of finding my own way."

And she swept out of the room.

Pat sat back down in the chair she'd been sitting

in. Her mother must be turning over in her grave at what she'd said to Aunt Liz. But she couldn't help it. Aunt Liz was a nosy old snoop, a born trouble-maker, who loved interfering in other people's lives because she didn't have enough in her own to keep her occupied.

And she was wrong about John being involved with Barbara. She had to be. Just because Aunt Liz was convinced about something didn't make it so.

Only why had Barbara been so constrained at lunch that previous Monday? If she truly was involved with John, that would explain it, wouldn't it?

It would also explain her turning red when Pat had said whatever she'd said about Barbara being a third person, somebody not involved in the situation. If she was involved . . .

The living room was chilly all of a sudden, and Pat hugged herself.

It would also explain why John had so hotly denied that he was interested in another woman. He wouldn't want her to think he was having an affair with Barbara behind her back.

Only why wouldn't he want her to think that if it were true? His carrying on with Barbara wouldn't upset her any more than his carrying on with somebody else.

And if Barbara wanted John, wouldn't she want him divorced and free to marry her? Wouldn't she insist he make a clean break with the past?

Pat hugged herself more tightly, but shivered anyhow. Whatever Aunt Liz might have to say about Barbara, Pat had always thought her direct and open. She still thought of her as that. However hard she tried, she couldn't picture Barbara sneaking around, having a back-street romance with somebody while trying to pretend that nothing at all was going on.

But if John wasn't involved with Barbara, then whom was he involved with?

Somebody had taken her place in his affections, that was certainly true. Somebody had made him change the way he felt about his wife.

And apparently for good, divorce or no divorce.

Pat burst into tears and sat there huddled in the chair, hugging herself, sobbing for what had been and what was now never to be again.

The phone rang, startling her the way the doorbell had earlier.

She let it ring. She wasn't in any condition to talk to anybody—or to have to explain why she was crying.

The phone kept ringing, on and on, as if demanding she answer it. She buried her face in her hands until finally the sound died away.

With a sigh Dave Gilchrist hung up the phone. He wondered where Pat was. He had tried to reach her on a number of occasions without any luck.

He was concerned about her. The last time he had seen her she hadn't looked at all well, her face white and drawn, a lackluster look in her blue eyes—a sure sign that she and John were still estranged.

He sighed again and made a mental note to keep on trying to reach Pat until he did so.

The phone was also ringing at the Cory residence. Rachel answered it, finding Iris at the other end of the line.

"Rachel, how are you?"

"I'm all right, Iris."

"Only 'all right'?"

Rachel made a face, but added brightness to her voice. "No, I'm fine. Thank you."

"There," Iris said, sounding satisfied. "That's much better. I was wondering, dear, if I might come by for a few minutes."

"It's all right with me, but Mac isn't here. He's at the office."

"On a Saturday afternoon?"

Rachel made another sour face. Iris could take the most innocent piece of information and turn it into something darkly significant. She was probably hoping Mac could no longer stand the sight of her and had departed for his office, even though nobody else was on the premises.

"He had some editorial work he wanted to do, Iris, and he figured with nobody there to interrupt him and the phones not constantly ringing, he could get something accomplished."

"Oh."

Pleased that for once she'd managed to take the wind out of Iris's sails, she went on to say, "But he probably won't mind too much if you call him there." The truth was, Rachel admitted to herself, he wouldn't mind at all. But then Iris probably already knew that.

"But it isn't my daddy I want to see. It's you."

"Me?" Rachel couldn't keep the surprise out of her voice.

"Yes, dear. So is it all right if I come by? I won't stay long."

"Well, of course it's all right. What do you want to see me about?"

"I'd rather not say on the phone."

Instantly Rachel was filled with foreboding. What was Iris up to now?

"You understand, dear. It's always much easier to talk in person. Especially when we're talking about something that matters."

"Yes," Rachel said. "I understand." But she didn't. She herself had always been able to talk on the phone to a person, whether it was about something that mattered or not. She couldn't think what Iris could have up her sleeve. And that made her more nervous than if she already had a clue.

"Is now a good time, dear?"

"Yes. Now is fine, Iris."

"I won't be interrupting *your* work, will I?" Iris's voice was positively silken.

"No. I wasn't working."

"Good. I'll be over as soon as I can get there. Good-bye, Rachel."

"Good-bye, Iris." Rachel hung up the telephone and picked up a magazine, but she was too keyed up to concentrate. Try as she would, she couldn't imagine what Iris wanted of her, only that it had to be something that would be to Iris's advantage, not hers. That was the only way Iris operated.

Rachel put the magazine aside and went to the big French windows at the back of the living room. She stood staring out at the rain and the wet sweep of lawn and the pink and white azaleas bordering it, their petals drooping under the rain's assault, however much the gardener claimed they needed the rain.

She was still standing there when the doorbell rang a few minutes later.

"I don't want to dribble rain into your house, dear," Iris said as she breezed into the foyer and took off her raincoat.

"It doesn't matter," Rachel said, for lack of knowing what else to say.

"Of course it matters. I wouldn't want anybody dribbling rain into my house." She opened the foyer closet and hung her coat in it, then turned to Rachel. "Now, my daddy told me the other day that you were working on a wonderful piece of sculpture, and I demand to see it."

"Well, sure, though I don't know how wonderful it is. When it comes to my work Mac always exaggerates." Rachel led the way to the room off the living room that she had converted into her studio. The piece Mac had been referring to was a little black horse and, secretly proud of it, she picked it up to show to Iris.

Iris took it from her and held it in her hands, admiring it. She shook her sleek blond head. "My daddy doesn't exaggerate. This is beautiful."

For once Iris sounded as if she sincerely meant

what she said. Rachel was so stunned she couldn't help saying, "Do you really mean that, Iris?"

"Of course I mean it. You have to stop denigrating yourself. You know, running yourself down."

Rachel had known, and she was amused that Iris always felt compelled to define her large vocabulary. But she said nothing, not wanting to start a confrontation.

Iris set the horse back down and went on admiring it. "When did you do this?"

"Since I've been home from the hospital."

"It's amazing. Truly amazing." She turned from the horse and, taking Rachel's arm, led her back into the living room, as if she were the hostess and Rachel the guest. "I'm delighted to see that you've recovered so beautifully."

"I do feel better every day," Rachel admitted.

Iris patted her hand, then went to sit on the sofa. "I'm sure you do, dear. It shows in the little black horse. It's as exquisite as anything you've ever done." She gave Rachel a small smile. "In my opinion, of course."

"But your opinion counts, Iris," Rachel said sincerely. Iris knew a lot about painting and sculpture.

"And it isn't only my opinion, Rachel. You're getting quite a reputation, you know."

Rachel flushed, as much with pleasure as embarrassment. "People have been kind. Most people anyhow. A few have said hurtful things."

Iris looked positively triumphant. "Which only proves what I just said about your reputation. The snipers don't bother with a Little Miss Nothing. If you didn't have talent, and I mean significant talent, they'd ignore you."

Rachel clasped her hands, her foreboding forgotten, the purpose of Iris's visit also forgotten. "Do you mean that?"

Iris nodded. "Of course I mean it." She beamed. "And that's why I'm here."

Memory flooded back. And with it confusion. What could Iris be up to where Rachel's artwork was concerned? She might want her to paint a picture for her or sculpt a piece for nothing so she could donate it to some charity. But surely it couldn't be that because that was something Rachel wouldn't mind at all doing.

"I don't understand, Iris. I mean about that being why you're here. Because of my reputation as an artist?" She shook her head. "I don't understand," she repeated.

"I have a surprise for you."

Rachel thought to herself that that much was obvious. At this point, whatever Iris came out with would be a surprise. "What kind of surprise?" she asked suspiciously.

"A nice one. At least I hope you'll think it's a nice one." She took a breath, and Rachel waited, her nerves beginning to jangle again. "I want to give you a new art studio."

Rachel stared at her in astonishment.

"I'll ask Robert to design it for you, with you having the final say, of course. And I'll have it built right here on your estate." Taking Rachel's arm again she led her to the French windows and pointed to the great gray beech tree a hundred yards or so behind the house. "I thought over there by that beech. What do you think?"

Rachel stared from the tree back to Iris. "I don't know what to think. I'm too stunned to think."

Iris smiled a benevolent smile. "Of course you are, darling, but isn't it a magnificent idea?"

"Yes. Yes, it is." And it was. That was the trouble. Why should Iris want to do something so magnificent for her?

Iris had never cared for her, though she had pretended to for a while, and Rachel had been too thick-headed to see that it was only pretense. Even now Iris sometimes pretended she cared for her —like right this minute, for instance—but it was never genuine.

And on top of everything else there was that whole business of Clarice and her baby and Iris's husband, Robert. Rachel had already had it out with Iris about that. Iris knew, whether or not she wanted to admit it, that all Rachel had to do was go to Mac with the information, and then Iris's good relationship to her father would be all washed up, as well as her marriage to Robert.

Was that why Iris wanted to build a studio for her—to keep her from doing that?

Rachel shook her head. It couldn't be. She would never hurt Mac intentionally and Iris's marriage to Robert was as good as washed up anyhow all on its own.

"Rachel," Iris said, pulling the same stunt on her that she'd played on Iris at the hospital, "why are you shaking your head?" She frowned. "You're not saying no to my gift, are you?"

"No," Rachel answered. "But I can't say yes either. Not right away. It's such a generous offer I'm overwhelmed by it. I'll have to think about it."

Iris smiled and pointed once more to the great gray beech. "While you're thinking about it, my dear, try to imagine it. Your own studio, completely separate from the house, and with every facility you will ever need. And with north light, too. Oh, I'm sure you'll say yes. I just know you will."

"It's very possible," Rachel said, "but I do have to think about it."

Iris glanced at her watch. "And I have to get back home, so I'll leave you to your thoughts." She smiled once more. "And your imagining."

Watching Iris drive off, Rachel thought how clever she was with all that talk about imagining. Turning from the front door, she went back to stand at the French windows again. She would love nothing better than to have her own separate studio. And if Robert designed it, it would be a marvel.

Rachel sighed. She felt like Eve being tempted by the apple. Or was it the serpent? Well, never mind which it was, that was how she felt.

And Iris probably knew that, too.

She wished she knew what Iris was up to, what Iris wanted of her.

Maybe Mac knew. Or if he didn't know, maybe he could guess.

She went to the telephone and dialed his office. He answered on the first ring.

"Mac, it's Rachel. I want to ask you something," she said without pausing for him to greet her.

"Ask away, darling."

"I—" She broke off. Whether or not Mac knew what Iris was up to, the very act of asking him would be to force him to take one side or the other, to either give in to Rachel's suspicions about Iris or dismiss them as only imaginings. She hated doing that to him. "Mac, I've changed my mind."

"About what you wanted to ask me?"

"Yes. Do you mind?"

"Not if it's not important."

She crossed her fingers. "It isn't." And, for all she knew, maybe it wasn't. "I'll see you at dinner, okay?"

After hanging up the phone Rachel pondered the problem of what to do. She had to talk to somebody smarter than she was, somebody who could maybe see through Iris. She snapped her fingers. John Randolph. Perfect. He didn't like Iris, and he certainly saw through her. Maybe he could figure out what she was up to.

She dialed Information for his number, then called him.

He answered with a growl. "Yes?"

"Oh, John, it's Rachel. I'm sorry. I've called at a bad time, haven't I?"

"It's all right. What can I do for you?"

Whatever he said, he didn't sound as if it were all right, and she was tempted to apologize again and get off the phone. But she squared her shoulders and stuck out her chin. "I know it's the weekend and all, and I'm sorry to bother you with anything, but could I come to your office Monday morning to talk to you about a problem I've got? I mean, I'd pay you and all. I mean, like I was a client."

"Don't worry about that. Call Gloria first thing Monday and tell her I said to fit you in somewhere."

"Oh, that's perfect, John. I'll see you Monday. And thanks so much."

Once again Rachel hung up the phone. John had sounded a little better by the end of the conversation, but not much. She wondered what was the matter with him, then shrugged. Everybody seemed to have problems. She only hoped he could help to fix hers.

Chapter Six
Invitations and Discoveries

His confrontation with Pat left John in a black mood, and as the afternoon wore on his mood didn't improve. He tried watching a basketball game on television, but he couldn't bring himself to care for either team. Why he had said the things he had to her he didn't know. No wonder she had looked at him as if he were a stranger. He was beginning to wonder if he knew himself.

More than once he picked up the phone to call her and apologize, but each time he cradled it again before even starting to dial the familiar number. In their emotional state an apology from him could only lead to their reconciliation, and that was something he wasn't yet ready for.

He showered and shaved and dressed for dinner, then drove out to his country club.

A bad mistake. Saturday night at the club was dinner-dance night. The place was full of couples

—young, old, middle-aged. John ate a hamburger in the bar and left for home as quickly as he could.

The black mood was still with him Sunday morning. He went to church, but not to the one he and Pat belonged to. He couldn't risk running into her.

Instead he ran into Barbara.

She looked especially lovely, wearing a figured silk in different shades of pink—rose, fuchsia, and a pink so pale it was almost white. It was a close-fitting dress, showing off her magnificent figure, and to top it off she wore a wide-brimmed picture hat accented with a bunch of lifelike peonies. The effect was stunning.

Barbara was with an older woman John didn't know, so he didn't try to engage her in conversation, but only smiled and waved from across the church. Going home afterward he couldn't get her out of his mind, and finally he picked up the phone and called her.

"You looked magnificent at church this morning."

"Thank you, John. I didn't know you went to that church."

"I don't usually. Let me take you to dinner tonight."

"Oh, I don't know. Have you talked to Pat?"

"Yes, I have. Yesterday afternoon. Let me take you to dinner, and I'll tell you all about it."

There was a small silence at the other end, and then she said, "Am I going to like hearing what you have to say?"

Soaps & Serials™ Fans!

★ Order the *Soaps & Serials*™ books you have missed in this series.

★ Collect other *Soaps & Serials*™ series from their very beginnings.

★ Give *Soaps & Serials*™ series as gifts to other fans.

...see other side for ordering information

Soaps & Serials™
From Pioneer Communications
Network, Inc.

You can now order previous titles of **Soaps & Serials**™ Books by Mail!

Just complete the order form, detach, and send together with your check or money order payable to:

Soaps & Serials™
120 Brighton Road, Box 5201
Clifton, NJ 07015-5201

Please circle the book #'s you wish to order:

(A) The Young and The Restless........	1	2	3	4	5	6	7	8	9	10
(B) Days of Our Lives....	1	2	3	4	5	6	7	8	9	10
(C) Guiding Light........	1	2	3	4	5	6	7	8	9	10
(D) Another World......	1	2	3	4	5	6	7	8	9	10
(E) As The World Turns..	1	2	3	4	5	6	7	8	9	10
(F) Dallas™	1	2	3	4	5	6	7	8	9	10
(G) Knots Landing™.....	1	2	3	4	5	6	7	8	9	10

Each book is $2.50 ($3.50 in Canada).

Total number of books circled_____ × price above = $ _____

Sales tax (CT and NY residents only) $ _____

Shipping and Handling $ _____.95

Total payment enclosed $ _____
(check or money orders only)

Name _____

Address _____ Apt# _____

City _____

State _____ Zip _____

Telephone (_____) _____
                Area Code

AW 10

"Yes."

"You're sure?"

"Yes, I'm sure. So how about it?"

"All right. But I have a better idea. Instead of you taking me out, why don't you come here for dinner?"

"Oh, Barbara, I don't want to put you to a lot of trouble."

"It won't be. It will be fun. I love cooking, and I especially love it when I have somebody to cook for that I care about."

"Well, if you're sure."

"Darling, yes. Come at six."

"All right. I'll see you then."

John cradled the phone, the sound of her "darling" still ringing in his ears, his black mood returning. What had made him say she would like hearing what he had to say about his meeting with Pat?

Because she wouldn't have agreed to have dinner with him otherwise, he admitted ruefully.

He walked over to the window that overlooked the quiet, residential street and stared out of it. He was being unfair to Barbara, giving her ideas she shouldn't be given, and maybe giving her hope as well.

Who was he kidding? he thought. There was no maybe about it. If Barbara were only interested in having an affair with him she wouldn't be so concerned about his marital situation. She had made it quite clear that marriage was her goal.

Well, there was no way she was going to achieve

that, not with him, and the sooner he told her that, the better. The truth was he didn't want to make a permanent break from Pat. Childish as it might seem, he simply wanted to give her a taste of her own medicine, let her see how it felt to be the disregarded one, the one left holding the bag.

John turned from the window. He would level with Barbara tonight. It would make the evening a sticky one. And the next few days at the office might be a bit hard to take as well. But the courthouse business would be coming to trial this next week, and that would keep both of them busy. And by the time the trial was over, the two of them would be back on an even keel again, their one night of impetuosity forgotten.

So saying this, he felt better. And feeling better, he drove out to the country club and played a round of golf.

While John was playing golf Barbara was getting everything ready for dinner that evening. Robbed of her earlier opportunity to cook dinner for him, she was doubly pleased to be doing it today. She even managed to put together the same menu —filet mignon, baked potatoes, a tossed green salad. And since the German bakery was closed on Sunday she made a lime mousse for dessert.

She had cleaned her apartment the day before, so it was already sparkling. While she was out buying her groceries she stopped at a florist shop and bought some red and pink tulips for the coffee table. It was a pity he couldn't have even so much as a glass of wine. There was something romantic about sharing wine before dinner. Well, she would simply have to make do with candlelight. It, too, was romantic.

An hour before he was due to arrive she took a long and lazy bubble bath, the air as well as the water filled with a spicy fragrance. Then she dressed, putting on the same dress she had worn to church that morning since he admired it so much, taking special care with her hairdo, brushing and patting it into the right arrangement.

Finally she was ready. She looked around her attractive living room, checked the red and pink tulips, the candles waiting to be lighted. It was going to be a wonderful evening.

Dave Gilchrist spent Sunday afternoon at his office, working on patient files, bringing them up to date. He would be glad when everything was put on computers, and each patient's records could be summoned up with a punch of a few buttons.

Halfway through the stack on his desk, he reached for the phone to try Pat again. He still hadn't gotten through to her, and now he was beginning to worry.

To his surprise, and relief, she answered the phone.

"Pat," he said, "Dave Gilchrist. I don't know how many times I've tried to get you in the last few days. I was beginning to get alarmed."

"I'm sorry, Dave," she said. "There isn't anything to get alarmed about. I've just been in and out a lot, I guess. How are you?"

"I'm fine. It's you I want to know about. How are you?"

"I'm okay."

He frowned into the phone. "Are you sure?"

She sighed. "Well . . ."

"Have you and John been talking?"

"If you can call it that. I saw him yesterday."

"And?"

"He can't be budged. Or at least I wasn't able to budge him." She sighed again. "I can't understand him. He doesn't want a reconciliation, and he doesn't want a divorce. Or so he says, anyhow. Can you understand that?"

"No, I can't, Pat. How did the two of you leave things? I mean, when you finished talking?"

"I'm afraid when we finished we weren't talking," she said wearily. "We were shouting."

"I'm sorry."

"Yes. So am I. For all the good it's likely to do me."

Dave evened the corners of the remaining stack of patient files. "Do you still want a reconciliation?"

"Yes."

"Then, I think you'll get it."

"Where does the cheery forecast come from?"

"It's just a feeling I have. Look, Pat. I'm here at the office tending to some paperwork. I'll be here for another hour or so. How about having dinner with me when I'm finished?"

"Well . . . all right. Why not?"

"Wonderful. How's six o'clock?"

"Fine."

"Good. I'll pick you up then."

Cradling the phone, Dave attacked the remaining files with gusto. After he heard in detail tonight what Pat had to say about her confrontation with John yesterday, then maybe he could talk John into having dinner with him one night this coming week and try to help them resolve their differences. It was worth a try anyhow.

Hanging up the phone, Pat shook her head, surprised she had accepted his dinner invitation so readily. Then she asked herself, Why not? Dave was a good friend as well as her physician. She didn't know anybody she could talk to more easily. And maybe in talking to him she could figure out what was going on with John. Or maybe Dave could.

She went upstairs to take a shower and get dressed.

She was just coming downstairs when the front door opened and her son, Michael, came in carrying a textbook. He gave her a big smile. "Hey, Mom, you look terrific! What's up?"

"I'm going out for dinner." Reaching her son, she kissed him on the cheek. "To what do I owe this unexpected visit?"

"Are you going with Dad?" he asked, ignoring her question.

Michael looked so much like his father in that moment Pat could have wept. He had his father's athletic, somewhat stocky build, and the same sensitive face with the full mouth and the dark eyes. Pat shook her head. "No, darling, I'm afraid not. I wish it were so, but it isn't."

"Who, then?"

"I'm having dinner with Dr. Gilchrist."

The remnants of his smile disappeared, and his mouth turned sulky. "You told me you wanted to make things up with Dad."

Pat nodded. "I do want to."

"Then why are you dating somebody else?"

Pat put a hand out to him. "Darling, I'm not dating Dave Gilchrist."

"Then what do you call it?" he asked, noting "Doctor" had been replaced with "Dave."

"I call it having dinner with a friend. And that's all it is."

"Maybe that's all it is to you."

"That's all it is to Dave, too."

A frown was added to the sulkiness. "And where are you going to have dinner?"

Pat shrugged. "I don't know. Some restaurant here in the city. What difference does it make?"

The frown became a scowl. "Well, what about all the people who see you and Dr. Gilchrist having dinner together? What will they think?"

Pat stroked her son's face. "I don't know what they'll think, Mike. Or if they'll think anything. Anybody who knows us knows that Dave is my doctor and my friend."

Michael shrugged away from her. "And what if word of it gets back to Dad?"

Now Pat frowned. "And what if it does? Your

father also knows what my relationship is to Dave Gilchrist. And he certainly knows that Dave has been trying to reconcile the two of us. So if he thinks anything, he'll think the truth—that Dave asked me to have dinner with him to talk about the problems your father and I are having and to see if he can do something more to get us back together again."

Mike looked unconvinced. "Maybe."

Once again Pat put a hand out to him. "Darling, what can I say to convince you? Dave called here in the first place to see how I was. He'd been trying to reach me the last few days and hadn't been able to, and he was concerned about me."

Once again Michael shrugged away from her. "I spent all last week trying to get hold of Glenda. And for the same reason."

"Well, yes, but—"

He cut her off. "But what? What's the difference?"

"You and Glenda go out together."

He put his hands on his hips in a challenging gesture. "And what do you call what you and Dr. Gilchrist are doing tonight if it's not going out together?"

Pat sighed. "You are taking words and twisting them to make them mean something they don't. Yes, Dave and I are going out together this evening. To have dinner. Period. We are not going out in the sense that you and Glenda go out. We are not dating or having an affair or even a romance. We are friends. And he is a particularly supportive friend." She sighed again at the still-unconvinced look on her son's face. "The reason we're having dinner together is to talk about your father and what Dave or I or anybody else we can think of can do to get your father to come back to me. Now, does that satisfy you?"

"I guess," Michael said, but he didn't look satisfied.

"Try to be civil to him when he gets here, will you?"

"What time is he coming?"

"At six."

"With luck I won't be here when he gets here. I'm supposed to help Marianne do some research at the library this evening. It closes at seven."

"She called from Boston to say she won't be home until tomorrow."

"Oh. Well, maybe I'll stick around here and do some studying. It's less distracting than my apartment."

"So do try to be civil to him. Okay?"

He nodded. "Okay, Mom."

For his mother's sake Michael did try to be civil to Dr. Gilchrist, and he guessed he managed it okay. There didn't seem to be any tension in the air. The doctor came in to the house pleasant, and he went out again pleasant.

Looking after them, Mike stood in the doorway after they left. They hadn't acted like anything was going on between them. Of course, his mother had fair warning, and Dr. Gilchrist being a doctor, he could probably put on a front easier than most people. Doctors were always keeping things hidden from their patients, weren't they? Telling them everything was going to be all right when just the opposite was true.

Still, why would his mother want to get involved with Dr. Gilchrist or anybody else if she really did want his dad to come back to her?

Michael sighed. Parents were good at keeping things from their kids, too. Especially things they didn't want them to know or thought weren't good for them to hear. Maybe his mom was only saying she wanted his dad to come back home. Maybe she was actually thinking of divorcing him, and maybe that was what she wanted to talk to Dr. Gilchrist about.

He shook his head. He wished he could think of what to do to keep that from happening. Maybe he could talk to Barbara. She worked with his dad and ought to know what he was thinking. She certainly knew what he was like by this time. And from that kind of knowledge she ought to know what it would take to get his dad to come home again.

Realizing he couldn't concentrate on his studies until this matter was more settled in his mind, he called Barbara to see if she was home and could maybe talk to him tonight. The line was busy.

He read a few pages of his text, then tried again. Still busy. Well, at least that meant she was home. He decided he'd just go on over there. If she didn't have time for him tonight he could set up a time with her later in the week.

Somebody was coming out of her building when he went up the front steps, and he caught the lobby door before it could close on him, so he didn't have to buzz her apartment from downstairs.

Walking down the carpeted hallway to her sixth-floor apartment, he heard music coming from her place. She answered his ring right away, saying as she opened the door, "This must be the, oh, Mike."

"Hi, Barbara," he said, figuring she must have company and wouldn't want to talk to him now. Then he saw who the company was. His father.

She opened the door wider. "Come in, Mike."

He went in assuming they must be working together on a case. Why else would his father be there? But then he saw how dressed up Barbara was, and he noted the candlelight in the room and the glass of wine in Barbara's hand and the smell of dinner cooking.

And the shocked look on his father's face at sight of him, the shock turning fast to guilt.

His father had been reclining on the sofa. Now he scrambled to his feet, saying, "Well, Michael, what a surprise."

Barbara was looking guilty, too, but she tried a smile and said, "I was just having a glass of wine with your father while we talked business. Won't you join us?"

Michael waved a hand around the room. "You call this business? Candlelight, flowers, music, wine. What do you think I am, stupid?"

His dad put out a hand to him, much like his

mom had done at home earlier. "Mike, don't jump to conclusions."

He spun to his father. "Why shouldn't I? Aunt Liz was right about the two of you, wasn't she? Instead of calling her an old snoop you should have admitted she knew what she was talking about."

"Mike," Barbara said.

Not staying to hear what she intended to say, he turned and left, slamming the door shut after him.

John would have gone after Michael, but Barbara argued against it. "He'll never listen to you. He's too upset."

"But I want to explain."

She spread her hands. "Explain what? I tried that and you saw how that worked. Give him time to cool down, and then tell him the truth: you were here to have dinner with me."

He frowned at her. "And?"

She shrugged. "And nothing."

"And do you think he'll believe that?"

"Probably not. But the only thing he has proof of is that you were here to have dinner."

"He doesn't care about proof."

"No, I don't suppose he does," she agreed. She sat down on the sofa and patted the cushion beside her. "Come back and sit down. I'm sorry Mike walked in on us, but it could have been worse, I suppose."

He made a face. "I don't see how." But he came back and sat down beside her.

She put a hand on his arm. "Your children are

no different from anybody else's. Of course they're upset by your separation from Pat, but in time they'll adjust."

He turned to her. He had come here prepared to level with Barbara. He just hadn't gotten to it, that was all, before Mike walked in on them. Well, the time had come now. "About that, Barbara," he began, then hesitated, searching for just how to put it in the least hurtful way.

"You did settle things with Pat, didn't you?" she asked.

He swallowed. He shouldn't have sat down so closely to her. She was tantalizing.

"Didn't you?" she repeated.

He swallowed again. "Yes, I did."

"And is everything all right? I mean, does Pat understand that you want the marriage ended?"

It wasn't too late. He could still level with her. If only she hadn't put her hand on his arm. If only she hadn't worn the perfume she was wearing. If only she didn't look the way she did. If only . . .

"Yes," he said, putting his conscience aside. "She understands that."

"And she didn't object?"

"No. She feels the same as I do—if one person wants out of a marriage, then what's the point of the other person trying to hang on to it."

Barbara nodded. "Very sensible. So it was an amicable meeting you had with her?"

John nodded. "Yes. And an amicable parting agreement. She'll work through a lawyer, of course."

"Well, yes, of course," Barbara agreed. "It's always much better that way." She picked up her wineglass and toasted him. "Oh, darling, how wonderful for us."

He let her take one sip to seal the toast. Then he took the glass from her and set it on the table and gathered her into his arms. He wanted her as much as he had ever wanted anything, and he meant to have her. Now.

After Michael stormed out of Barbara's apartment, he didn't know where to go or what to do. He was too keyed up to go home, and too distraught to study.

Leaving Barbara's building he set off down the street, not even paying attention to the direction he was taking. He wasn't dressed for running, but he started running anyhow. At first he ran according to the traffic lights and signs. If the light or the sign was against him, he simply turned in another direction. But eventually he saw that he was near Blackstock Field, and he headed there, running laps around its running track until he could run no longer. Then, panting, gradually decreasing his pace, he decided to stay at his mother's home that night. He desired the security the home of his youth offered; his apartment never felt like home.

He was glad now that Marianne had stayed another night in Boston, and he was hoping he would beat his mother home. That way he wouldn't have to face her until tomorrow.

But luck wasn't with him. His mother was standing in the foyer hanging her coat up in the closet.

"Back so soon?" he said.

She smiled. "Dinner can only last so long."

Immediately he was reminded of his father and Barbara. Of course dinner could only last so long. And then what? But he didn't have to ask himself that. He already knew the answer. Or at least the probable answer.

"Why are you here?" his mother asked him.

"I decided to stay the night, if that's okay?"

She smiled again. "You know this will always be your home. You don't have to ask permission."

He swallowed, wondering if it would ever really be home again. "Did you have a nice dinner?"

"Yes. Very nice." Pat closed the closet door and headed into the living room, her son following. "We drove out to the country club."

Michael frowned. "Weren't a lot of your friends there?"

"No, actually not. The place was pretty empty. But I told you earlier, darling, it didn't matter whether friends saw us or not. Dave and I have nothing to hide. We spent almost the entire time talking about your father."

The words were out before he could stop them. "For all the good that probably did."

"What's that supposed to mean?" she asked, frowning.

"Nothing."

She looked more closely at him. "Mike, has something happened?"

"No." He said it almost hopelessly. He was a rotten liar. His mother saw through him every time.

Apparently not this time. She shrugged and went to sit on the sofa, picking up the Sunday paper. "I meant to finish this earlier," she said, "but I didn't."

That was an old joke around their house, how his mother never could finish the Sunday paper because it was too fat. Thinking of it now made him want to cry.

He crossed the room to a chair opposite the sofa and plopped down in it. How his father could think Barbara had a nice place to live when he compared it to this home, Mike didn't know.

His mother looked up from the paper to frown at him. "What's the matter, Mike?"

He shook his head and lied again. "Nothing."

He must be getting better at it. All she said to that was, "Do you want part of the paper?"

"No, thanks. I've seen all of it I want to."

She went back to the section she was reading. "Oh," she said a minute later, "this must be the meeting Dave was referring to."

"What meeting?" Mike asked.

"On endocrinology." His mother put the paper down again. "It has to do with glands and body secretions. You know. Like the thyroid. Anyhow," his mother added, "this meeting is a dinner on Wednesday night over in Southport. Dave asked me if I'd like to drive over there with him for it."

"What did you tell him?"

"I said it was kind of him to ask me, but I didn't think I'd go."

"Why not?"

His mother stared at him. "Why not? You're asking me why not? The same young man who less than three hours ago was upset that I was even having dinner with Dave? And now you want to know why I won't go to a dinner meeting with him? I don't understand you."

"Well, maybe I've changed my mind."

She made a little grimace. "Your mind or your tune. One or the other." She went back to the paper.

"Mom, I'm serious."

Without looking up she said, "About what?"

"Your going out with Dr. Gilchrist."

She put the paper aside. "Michael, we're going to have to have some give and take about word usage. Even if I had told Dave I would go to this medical meeting with him Wednesday night I would not consider that 'going out' with him, as you put it."

"Well, I'm saying consider it."

She was staring incredulously at him again. "Why?"

He tried to shrug, though his inner turmoil was building up in him again. "Why does there have to be a why? Just do it."

"Did something happen to you tonight between

the time I left here and the time I got back?" When his only response was a shake of the head, she studied his face. "Why were you out?"

"What does that have to do with anything? I was out running. I run all the time."

"Not dressed the way you were."

"I didn't plan ahead of time, that's all. I didn't have my gear with me when I started."

"Where were you when you started running?"

"I was out."

"Out where?"

"Just out."

"Doing what?"

"I wasn't doing anything."

She frowned. "Then why were you out?"

Michael jumped to his feet. "Why do I have to answer all these questions? All I said was you should consider going out with Dr. Gilchrist. Not just consider it. Go out with him. And not just Dr. Gilchrist. Go out with other men. Go out with anybody you want to, see anybody you want to. Except for Barbara." He cringed when he realized what he had just let slip out.

His mother was back to staring at him. "Barbara? Barbara Weaver?"

"Yes."

"What do you mean?"

"I mean stay away from her."

His mother got to her feet. "Why should I stay away from her?"

"Because I said so, that's why," he shouted irrationally.

Before she could say anything more or put out a hand to stop him, he ran from the living room, up the stairs, and into his bedroom. He closed and locked the door behind him, then threw himself onto the bed, burying his head under the pillow so his mother couldn't hear him crying.

Chapter Seven
Truth

Pat stood in the living room listening to Michael
thunder up the stairs and down the hall, then slam
the door to his room. She started to go after him,
but changed her mind. Whatever had happened,
and something must have, he was far too upset to
talk about it now. She would let him sleep on it,
then talk to him about it in the morning. She sat
back down on the sofa to tackle the rest of the
Sunday paper once again, but as usual didn't finish
it before going upstairs to bed herself.

The next morning, as soon as she had showered
and dressed, she walked down the hall to her son's
bedroom. The door was open, but Mike wasn't
there. She hurried downstairs. He wasn't there
either; nor had he eaten breakfast. There were no
dishes in the sink. He obviously had gotten up and
dressed and left the house before she ever woke up.
Quietly, so she wouldn't hear him. He obviously
didn't want to talk to her—didn't want to answer
the questions he knew she wanted to ask.

Still trying to figure out what could have happened, Pat puttered about the kitchen, putting together breakfast for herself. As tempting as the food was, she had no appetite for it, and had to force herself to eat it. Over a second cup of coffee, she tried to recall exactly what Michael had said the previous night. It was hard to remember any of it, it had come as such a shock to her.

From not wanting her to have anything to do with Dave Gilchrist, Mike now was encouraging her to go out with him. And other men, too. Was it possible Mike had met with his father last night, that John had been more forthcoming with his son than he had been with her? Or maybe Mike had interpreted something John had said as meaning his father wanted out of the marriage permanently, so he didn't see any reason why his mother should shut herself up at home.

But why the remark about Barbara? Why had Mike told her to stay away from her?

Could Mike have seen John and Barbara somewhere together last night?

The only eating place she could think of where John and Mike might run into each other was the country club, and that was where she had been last night with Dave.

Where else?

Maybe nowhere else. Maybe John had taken Barbara out for dinner last night, and Michael had seen them in the car together, passed them in the street. That would explain why he had been running in his street clothes.

But it didn't explain why he had been upset enough to do so.

Why would simply seeing his father and Barbara in John's car make Mike jump to the conclusion that that meant the end of his parents' marriage? John and Barbara had had dinner together on a number of occasions in the past, particularly when they were working together in court.

Maybe Mike had gone to John's apartment to see his father and had found Barbara there with him. Maybe that was it. Only there had to be more to it than that. Could he have found them in some compromising position together, or thought he had?

Pat shook her head and finished her coffee. That would mean that Barbara was indeed involved with John, that in spite of her open nature she was taking part in a back-street relationship with him, was maybe having an affair with him. And maybe that was what Michael had walked in on.

She shook her head again. She had no proof of anything of the kind. All she had was a vivid imagination, a son with possibly an even more vivid imagination, and a desperation afflicting both her son and herself.

Sitting there conjecturing like this, she thought, she was putting herself on a level with Aunt Liz, letting her mind be poisoned in the same way. The only difference between them was that she wasn't on the telephone spreading her conjectures around town.

Well, she would stop conjecturing. She was

being unfair to Barbara. In fact, she would call her and make a lunch date.

The line was busy the first few times she tried it. She wasn't surprised. Monday was always a busy morning in John's office, and though he had two lines he really needed more. Pat made a note to say something to him about it before remembering he was no longer around for her to say such things to.

Swallowing the ache of disappointment, she tried the office again and this time got through. "It's Pat, Gloria. May I speak to Barbara, please?"

"Yeah, sure," Gloria said. "Hold on."

In a moment there was a click, and Barbara came on the line. "Yes, Pat. Good morning."

"Good morning, Barbara. How are you?"

"I'm fine, thank you." There was a lilt in Barbara's voice. A lilt of happiness. "How are you, Pat?"

"Fine, thanks." Barbara surely wouldn't be talking this way with her if she was carrying on with John behind her back. It wasn't possible. "I was calling to ask if we could get together for lunch one day this week."

"Oh, dear, I'm afraid not. Much as I'd like to."

"You're all dated up?"

"No, it isn't that. It's the courthouse trial. Jury selection begins tomorrow already."

"That soon?"

"Yes. You know how it is once a case comes to trial. You never know when you'll be free for lunch. Or sometimes dinner, either."

"Yes, I know." And she did. How many times over the years had John been tied up in court? Too many times to count. And times she might not ever have again. Once again the pain of disappointment rose up in her. And once again she had to swallow it down. "Well, I'm sorry, Barbara."

"Yes, I am, too. I hate to have to put you off until the case is over, but it looks as if I'll have to."

"That's all right. I understand."

"Good. Well, nice talking to you, Pat."

"Same here. Good-bye, Barbara."

Pat hung up the phone and stood looking at it, that same ache flooding through her now. She would never have believed it possible that she and John could have become as estranged as this, still couldn't believe it was happening, still felt as though she was trapped in some nightmare from which she hoped she would soon wake up.

When Pat's call came in, Barbara had been answering yet another offer of employment, this time from a law firm in Gary, Indiana. The call finished, she turned around to her typewriter to continue the letter turning down the offer, but sat for a few minutes with her hands resting on the keys.

She was sorry she'd had to turn down Pat's invitation for lunch. Not that she was exactly looking forward to getting together with her, but there were some things they had to say to each other, and the sooner they were said, the better. No matter how amicable Pat and John's separation agreement had been, Barbara still felt as though she was taking John away from Pat, and she needed to hear Pat say she understood, maybe even approved.

Pat was not the dog in the manger type, so she might very well approve. In any event, Barbara needed to hear for herself that Pat was not standing in the way.

Since the courthouse case wasn't starting until tomorrow she could have met Pat for lunch that day. She had told her friend Eva she'd have lunch with her, but she could break that date. Eva wouldn't mind.

Barbara picked up the phone and dialed Pat's number. The phone rang and rang with no answer. Finally Barbara broke the connection. Pat must have gone out. Well, too bad. She'd have to arrange something later. She picked up the phone again and called Eva to confirm their lunch date.

Over the roar of the washing machine Pat thought she heard the phone ringing. She listened intently. Yes, it was. She raced up the basement stairs to the kitchen phone, but when she picked it up all she got was a dial tone.

Disappointed, wondering who it had been, she went back down to the basement. John had been after her for years to have an extension put down there, but she had regarded it as a needless expenditure and had resisted doing it.

She shook her head. No matter what happened today—or didn't happen, as with the phone just now—it made her think of John. Surely he must have had some second thoughts about their bitter confrontation Saturday. Surely he couldn't have lost all feeling for her. Maybe he regretted what he had said to her. Maybe he wanted to meet with her again. Maybe that had been John calling her just now wanting to set up another meeting.

Was she letting her imagination run away with her again? Probably.

She went back to sorting through the second load of laundry, and again she heard the phone ringing. She raced up the stairs a second time, and this time she made it.

"Hello, Mom?"

Pat swallowed her disappointment, and the guilt that went with being disappointed that it was her daughter. "Yes, darling. Where are you?"

"I'm still in Boston. That's why I'm calling—to say I won't be home tonight. I want to spend at least another day here, and maybe two or three, if that's okay with you."

"As long as you're not wearing out your welcome, yes, that's all right."

"Mom, what about Dad? Are things still—you know."

"Yes, I'm afraid they are."

"Do you want me to come on home today, then, like I said I would?"

"No, that's not necessary. Take your time. And, Marianne, did you call here just a few minutes ago?"

"No. Why?"

"It's nothing. Somebody called, and I didn't get to the phone in time."

"It was probably a wrong number. See you in a couple of days, Mom."

Pat hung up and started back down to the basement, then changed her mind and went back to the phone. Maybe that had been John calling her, and maybe it hadn't been, but there was nothing to prevent her from calling him and asking for another meeting with him.

She dialed the office, and when Gloria answered the phone, she said, "It's Pat again. This time I'd like to speak to John if he's free."

"He's on the other line, Mrs. Randolph. Do you want to hold?"

"Yes, please."

Pat expected Gloria to put her on hold, but she left her on the open line. In a moment or two she heard the office door open and Rachel Cory's voice saying, "I'm here for my appointment with Mr. Randolph."

Gloria said, "Yes, Mrs. Cory. If you'll just take a seat he'll be with you in a moment." She came back on the line. "Mr. Randolph is off the other line now. Let me see if he can speak to you."

This time Gloria put her on hold, and Pat wondered what Rachel was seeing John about. More trouble with Iris, she would bet, but what help John could be to her where Iris was concerned she didn't know.

A click, and John came on the line. "Yes, Pat. What can I do for you?"

Pat tried to read his mood from the tone of his voice but couldn't. "I'd like to meet with you."

"We met on Saturday."

Not the response she had hoped for. Swallowing for courage, she said, "We didn't accomplish much of anything."

"No," he agreed, "we didn't."

A better response. Maybe if she backed off a little. "I just had a call from Marianne in Boston. She asked about you." Pat swallowed again. "Mike and Marianne both miss you, John."

"I miss them."

"Maybe after Marianne gets home we could all have dinner together here at the house."

"It's a possibility."

"Would you like that?"

"Pat, I don't know what I would like." Now he sounded exasperated. "If Michael and Marianne miss me so much, tell them to come and see me. They know where I live."

"I'm sorry," Pat said hastily. "I didn't mean to put you on the spot."

"Well, mean it or not, you did. Look, Pat, I can't talk any longer now. I've got a client waiting. I'll have to get back to you."

Without so much as a good-bye he broke the connection.

Rachel went into John's office. She'd been here so many times in the past, it held many memories for her, not all of them good. And this wasn't a good time for her either, though her visit today bore no relationship to those long-ago times. And for that, at least, she could be thankful.

"Sit down, Rachel," John said, greeting her.

"It's good of you to take the time for me," Rachel said. She sat in the chair opposite his desk. John looked harried. He was neatly dressed, as always, his tie straight, his jacket pressed, but his brown hair needed combing and he had an impatient air about him.

"How can I help you, Rachel? You said something on the phone to me Saturday about having a problem."

She pushed her dark hair back from her face. "It's Iris."

John scowled. "If you'd given me three guesses, chances are I could have come up with it. What's Iris done now?"

"She hasn't done anything yet. It's what she wants to do. She wants to give me a studio."

John gave her a look of noncomprehension. "An art studio?"

Rachel nodded. "Yes. I probably said something to her one time or another about wanting one. I mean, I've already got a makeshift studio in the house, but she wants Robert to design one for me that can be built in back of the house as a free-standing structure. And of course, as Iris pointed out, it would have every facility I could possibly want."

"And where does the problem come in?"

"The problem comes in letting her do it. I don't like taking things from Iris, things she wants to give me, I mean."

"I see," he said.

"But that's only part of the problem," Rachel added. "I mean, I expect you're sitting there thinking, well, if you don't want her to give you a studio, just say so. Politely, of course."

"I was thinking something along those lines," John said, nodding.

"The problem is," Rachel went on, "Iris already dislikes me. I mean, she pretends to like me, at least when it suits her purposes, but she doesn't. She's never forgiven me for marrying her father. So if I turn down her offer to give me a studio, that will give her still one more reason to be against me. And to run complaining to her daddy."

Rachel used the word "daddy" deliberately. She thought it was nauseating that a woman as grown-up and sophisticated as Iris still referred to her father as a four-year-old would.

"And," she added, "I don't want her running to Mac for his sake, too. I mean, he's always being put in the middle between us, having to choose to believe one or the other or side with one against the other. And it makes him terribly unhappy."

Rachel almost went on to say that Mac was already unhappy about something, though he kept denying it, but that was a separate problem. And anyhow, if she didn't know what it was, she couldn't expect John to know.

"Rachel," John said, interrupting her thoughts, "do you have any idea why Iris wants to give you this studio?"

"No. And I was just going to get to that. I mean, I don't understand it. I guess I shouldn't say this—and I hope you won't repeat it to anybody."

"No, Rachel. That's what lawyers are for, not to repeat things their clients tell them. And I regard you as a client."

She gave him a conspiratorial smile. "It sounds so elegant, doesn't it? Client."

He smiled back, though he still had the harried look about him. "Yes, it does. But to get on with what you were saying about Iris."

Rachel nodded. "Like I said, I probably shouldn't say this. I mean, it probably isn't very gracious of me, but I can't help feeling suspicious. I feel as if Iris is up to something." She sighed. "I guess I'm not smart enough to see what it is."

John leaned toward her. "You have no inkling?"

"No. None." She frowned at him. "Do you?"

"I think so, yes."

Rachel stared at him, astonished. While she was staring, he reached into his jacket pocket, took out a set of keys, and used one of the keys to unlock a drawer in his desk. He pulled out a long white envelope and handed it to her.

"Read what's in there," he said. "Then you'll understand what she's up to."

Still astonished, she opened the envelope and took out a sheet of paper covered with big, splashy handwriting. What she read astonished her further. And appalled her. She looked from the sheet of paper to John. "I knew I had called Iris. I knew I hadn't just dreamed I'd done it. Oh, how could I have let her talk me into believing it was only a dream?"

John shrugged. "You weren't in the best of shape physically or emotionally."

"No, I wasn't. But still . . ." She gave a shake of her head. "It's all coming back to me now. I called

Iris and asked to speak to Mac, and she wouldn't let me. She said he was tied up with Robert and couldn't be interrupted. Then she hung up on me, and I didn't have the nerve to call her back. The pains got worse, I passed out, and that put an end to it. Then I lost the baby."

"And," John put in, "it's probably Iris's fault that you did. At least she sees it that way, ergo the art studio."

Rachel couldn't believe it. Iris had not only caused her to lose her baby, she'd tried to put something over on her. Well, she hadn't gotten by with it this time.

And there was more in the splashy handwriting. She read the paragraph about Robert and Clarice and Iris, then looked at John, holding the sheet of paper out to him. "Where did this information come from?"

"A young woman named Tracey DeWitt. Do you know her?"

Rachel nodded. "Yes. She's a friend of Iris's, or was, apparently. And an old girlfriend of Mac's." She wrinkled her nose. "Iris had her here for a visit a little while ago hoping Mac would leave me and go back to Tracey. But it didn't work."

John put the document back in its envelope and returned it to the drawer. He explained how Tracey had come into his office. "She said she wanted it off her conscience."

"Well, she got what she wanted."

"Which is more than I can say for most of us."

Rachel didn't quite understand what he was

talking about, but before she had a chance to ask him to explain, he said, "Were you privy to this other information about Robert and Clarice?"

"Yes," she answered. "In fact I spent a whole day debating whether or not I should go to Mac with it, but I couldn't decide. If I did go to him, Mac would probably disown Iris, and when Robert found out why, their marriage would be all washed up. But if I didn't, then maybe Robert never would know the truth about how Iris had deceived him into marrying her." She sighed. "I was still trying to decide what to do when the pains started, and then I couldn't think about anything but that."

"I'm sorry I had to remind you of all that," John said.

She put a hand up. "It's all right. In some ways what's hardest about it is seeing that Iris is even meaner than I realized." She frowned. "What was it you said about her that time you came to see me in the hospital?"

"That she wasn't above using anybody or anything to get what she wanted for herself."

"That's right," Rachel said. "That's a perfect way of putting it." She shook her head. "And to think she thought she could buy me off by giving me a studio. The nerve!"

"The way a woman like Iris operates takes nerve," John agreed.

John's buzzer sounded, and he picked up the phone. "Yes, Gloria?" He listened, then glanced at his watch and said, "Ask him if I can get back to him in a few minutes." There was another short pause, and then he said, "All right, fine," before hanging up.

Rachel reached for her purse. "I know you're busy."

"That's all right," he said, putting his hand up. "Take all the time you need."

"I think I've taken it all already, except for deciding what to do about telling Mac. It's one thing to tell him how Iris deceived Robert into marrying her before he could find out about Clarice and her baby. Iris could claim she didn't know about it herself, and it would be her word against mine, or it would have been until Tracey gave you that piece of paper. But how can Iris wriggle her way out of that phone call I made to her?"

"I don't know," John said.

"And that's another thing," Rachel added. "Where Robert is concerned Iris could make up all kinds of things about being so crazy in love with him she wasn't thinking straight. Things that would put what she did in a better light. So Mac could make excuses for her, if he was looking to make them."

"And he probably would be," John agreed.

"Yes, he would," Rachel said. She spread her hands. "But what possible excuse will Iris have where the phone call is concerned? There wasn't any reason, not one that makes any sense, for her not to call Mac to the phone or at least tell him I had called and wanted him to call me. So what can she say to him?"

"I don't know," John answered. "But I suspect

that if she had been able to come up with something plausible, she wouldn't have had to resort to offering you the art studio."

"No," Rachel said. "That's right. She wouldn't have. I wish you could tell me what to do." She sighed. "I mean, do you see what my problem is?"

"I'm not sure, Rachel. Could you be a little more specific?"

"Well, if Iris isn't going to be able to wriggle her way out of the phone call thing, then that would mean Mac would be terribly angry with her, so angry he might never want to have anything more to do with her."

John nodded. "Yes, I can see that."

"And wouldn't that be a terrible thing for Iris, knowing how she feels about her father?"

"She should have thought of that when she refused to let you talk to him."

"I know, but . . ." Rachel's voice trailed off, and she sighed again. "I mean, do you understand the terrible pickle this puts me in?"

He nodded again. "I think I do, yes."

Once again his buzzer sounded, and once again he picked up the phone and listened as he had before. "I'll have to get back to her. I can't talk to her now."

Rachel wondered if it was Pat on the phone calling him, and she felt bad to be unburdening herself to him when he had problems of his own. She wished she could help him and Pat get back together, but she didn't know how.

John hung up the phone and turned back to her. "Now, you were saying . . ."

"I was saying what a pickle this puts me in, and you were agreeing with me. I mean, do I want to be the one who cuts Mac off from his only child?"

John picked up a pencil and toyed with it. "No, I'm sure you don't want to, Rachel, and I don't blame you."

She leaned toward him. "So what should I do?"

He was already shaking his head. "That's the one thing I can't advise you on. It's a decision you're going to have to make for yourself."

She sighed. He hadn't told her anything she didn't already know. Nor had she expected him to tell her what to do. It had been a wild hope that he might blurt out something that she could agree with and then act on before she lost her nerve.

She could hear the phone ringing again in the outer office and got to her feet. "I really can't take any more of your time. And no exceptions this time."

He stood up, too. "I hope I've been of some help."

She smiled. "Oh, you have. Now that I know what was behind her generous offer, I can tell Iris thanks, but no thanks."

John gave her a kindly look. "And Mac?"

She shrugged. "It's like you said, John. Nobody can make that decision for me. I've got to make it." She put a hand up. "So don't you worry about it. One of us worrying is enough."

"All right," he said. "But you'll let me know what happens."

"Yes, I will." She made a face. "Though if I

decide I will tell Mac, and he has it out with Iris, you might hear the explosion on your own."

John laughed and, waving a hand at him, Rachel walked out of his office. She left the building, undecided what to do. It was a lovely day outside, and she walked along the downtown street, window-shopping, reminded suddenly of the days before her marriage when window-shopping was the only kind of shopping open to her.

Why couldn't Iris accept her as Mac's wife? Why did she have to do all these terrible things to try to break up their marriage when none of them was going to accomplish that? Surely even Iris could see how happy Mac was with her.

Or had been with her.

What was eating away at Mac, making him unhappy?

She stood in front of a shop window, looking at a snappy tennis outfit. For a few moments she was tempted to go inside and buy it, but instead she sighed and continued on her way. Her heart wasn't in shopping today.

If she told Mac about the phone call, she thought, it could only make him unhappier than he already was. Maybe she should just keep quiet, let things be.

She couldn't decide.

Chapter Eight
Turning Points

Pat Randolph decided she had to do something. John had said he would get back to her, but he hadn't. She supposed with the press of work, especially with a case coming to trial, he had let it slip his mind. Well, then, he surely wouldn't hold it against her that she was reminding him.

She started toward the phone, then changed her mind. She could do a better job talking to him in person. She glanced at her watch. Almost one o'clock. John might be at lunch, but the chances were he was eating it at his desk. And Barbara might very well be eating with him if, as was usually the case, they were huddled together over the pretrial material they had amassed, checking the notes they had made on the potential jurors, getting everything set for tomorrow morning.

Halfway out the front door, Pat hesitated. Since John and Barbara probably would be conferring together, this probably wasn't a good time to try to talk to him. It might even irritate him to be interrupted. Better to pick a more auspicious time.

She would do a little shopping first, then go to the office, and by that time they would surely have finished their luncheon meeting and be back at their own desks again taking care of other clients and other matters.

Immediately she felt better. Getting into her car, she drove downtown, parked the car in a municipal parking lot, and headed for a department store.

Nearly an hour later she emerged from it with a new jacket to go with a skirt she had bought the week before. She took her package to the car, locked it in the trunk, and set off for the office.

Nobody was in the outer office. Either Gloria had gone out for a late lunch, or John had sent her to the courthouse with some papers to file.

The door to John's office was open, and at first nobody seemed to be there either. Then Pat looked over by the window and put her hand to her mouth to keep from gasping aloud.

John had Barbara in his arms and was kissing her passionately. And Barbara was kissing him back just as passionately. She pulled back and said in a low voice Pat had to strain to hear, "Darling, we can't. Gloria will be back any minute."

The sound of that "darling" and the way Barbara was talking to him—as if she'd said this to him many times before—sent shock waves through Pat's body.

Oh, Pat thought, *what a fool I've been.*

John was sighing with regret. "I know," he

murmured to Barbara, still holding her tightly in his arms. "But I just can't get enough of you."

She smiled at him. "You'll have all you want of me very soon." She pulled back farther from him. "You can wait."

He drew her to him again. "Oh, no, I can't."

"Then, at least tell me you love me."

He looked intently into her eyes. "Darling, I do love you. I just need time, that's all."

A little frown replaced Barbara's smile. "But you told me last night at my place that you and Pat had already reached an amicable separation agreement."

Another shock wave for Pat.

John sighed. "That's right, and we have, but these things take time. To work out all the details, I mean. You know how it is."

Barbara's frown did not smooth out. "But you did talk to her. And she did agree."

John nodded. "Yes, darling. Now come on. Just one more kiss before Gloria gets back."

Barbara tried to resist. At least that was how it looked to the horrified Pat, but after a moment or two she gave in to his entreaties, and once again they were locked in an embrace, the world shut out, totally oblivious to Pat's presence or, she suspected, to anything else.

She turned and tiptoed out of the office, not stopping until she was on the sidewalk, people shoving by her in either direction. She simply stood there as still as a stone, reliving the scene in John's office in her mind, telling herself over and over again what a fool she had been, what a terrible, terrible fool.

Eventually she made her way to the parking lot, though afterward she had no memory of doing so, and got in the car and drove home as if in a trance.

She went into the house and upstairs to her bedroom, where she shut the door and locked it. She didn't want to see anybody or hear from anybody. She wanted to be left alone. That was how John had left her, wasn't it? Alone, alone, alone.

It was almost four o'clock when Michael reached the house. He had spent most of the day mulling over what he would say to his mother when he got there. He knew he owed her an explanation for the things he had blurted out to her last night.

He shook his head. It wasn't that she didn't have the right to know. He just hated having to be the guy who told her.

Chin up, he said to himself as he let himself into the house.

"Mom?" he called out.

No answer. But he knew she was there. Her car was in the driveway. Unless she had gone to one of the neighbors for something.

"Mom?" he called again, going from room to room in the downstairs part of the house, then went upstairs. "Mom? It's Mike. Are you up here?"

He walked down the hall to her bedroom, saw that the door was closed, and knocked on it. "Mom? Are you in there?"

No answer. No sound.

He tried the door. It was locked. "Mom," he called again. "Let me in. Please. I've got to talk to you. At least let me know you're okay."

Still no answer. And still no sound.

He pounded on the door. "Mom, if you don't answer me I'll go down to the basement and get an ax and chop the door down. Mom, do you hear me?"

At last he got an answer. "Yes, I hear you, Michael. Go away." Her voice was so weak, he almost didn't recognize it.

"Mom, what's the matter?"

"Nothing's the matter. Go away. I don't want to talk to you. Nothing's the matter," she repeated feebly.

"Then why have you locked yourself in the bedroom?"

"Because I want to be left alone."

"Because of the things I said to you last night?"

"No."

"Don't you want to know why I said them?"

"No."

He didn't believe that. Unless . . . "Mom, did you talk to Dad today?"

She didn't answer him.

"Mom, did something happen today?"

Again there was no answer.

He was getting nowhere. He walked back down the hall and sat down on the top step of the stairs. His mom must have found out about his dad and Barbara. That had to be the reason she'd locked herself in her room and had refused to talk to him.

He tried to think what to do, who to turn to. Not his father, that was for sure.

And Aunt Liz was definitely out. His mother might forgive him for going to somebody for help, but she'd never forgive him if he went to Aunt Liz.

Mike snapped his fingers. Of course. Dr. Gilchrist. His mother would surely listen to him, and he already knew Mike's parents were separated, so she'd be saved that embarrassment.

Mike got up and headed for the phone downstairs. He would call Dr. Gilchrist and explain the problem to him. Surely he'd be willing to help.

After mulling her problem over—and window-shopping for several blocks while doing it—Rachel decided to take her problem to Dave Gilchrist. Whether or not he could fit her in, she didn't know.

The only way to find out was to go ask his nurse, who said if Rachel didn't mind waiting a few minutes the doctor could see her.

It was a lot more than a few minutes before the nurse said she could go in, but Rachel gave her a smile and entered, closing Dave's office door behind her.

He waved her to a chair. "Sit down, Rachel."

"Thanks, Dave."

The nurse had handed Dave her chart, and he had it open on his desk. Rachel shook her head. "You won't need the chart, Dave. There isn't anything wrong with me. I just need to talk to you if you have the time."

"All right." He closed her chart and folded his hands.

He was a nice man in addition to being a good doctor, she thought. She had always liked him. And he was nice-looking, too. Not that that was essential, but it didn't hurt any. He was tall and slender, with long, capable-looking hands, and a caring face with compassionate dark eyes.

He was looking at her now, intent upon her, ready to hear what she had to say. And, with luck, tell her what to do.

"It's about Iris," she said. She told him about the phone call and how Iris had tried to convince her she'd never made it, and how she had proof now that she had.

Concluding the story, Rachel spread her hands. "So now I've got this information backing me up, and I don't know what to do about it. Part of me says tell Mac, and part of me says don't tell him."

Dave frowned. "Why not tell him?"

"Because he's already unhappy about something. He says he isn't, but I know he is, and I don't want to add to his problems." She sighed. "I don't even like burdening you with this, but I can't work it out for myself."

Dave settled back in his chair. "I'm glad you came here, Rachel. I'm only sorry you didn't come to me sooner. I had no idea you didn't know."

Rachel frowned. "Didn't know what?"

"What's bothering Mac. I assumed he had told you."

She shook her head. "He hasn't told me anything. I've asked him over and over, and he just keeps saying it's nothing. You know what it is?"

"Yes. He feels it's his fault that you lost the baby."

"What?" Rachel stared at Dave wide-eyed. "Mac's fault?"

"Yes."

"But how could it possibly be his fault?"

"Because he was so late getting home that night."

Rachel was still wide-eyed with wonder. "But that wasn't his fault. That was Iris's fault. For not letting me talk to him."

Dave nodded. "That's right. And that's why you must tell him the truth about the phone call. Far from adding to his problems, it will relieve him of them."

"Except for having to deal with Iris about it."

Dave shrugged. "Yes, there is that. But that's between Mac and Iris. You can't do anything about that."

"No, I suppose not, but still . . ."

Dave gave her another of his intent looks. "You have to tell him. You have no choice."

"But—"

He shook his head, silencing her. "No buts, Rachel. You asked me for my advice. Now take it."

Before she could answer him, there was a knock at the door, and the nurse stuck her head in. "I'm sorry to bother you, doctor, but Mike Randolph is on the phone asking for you. He says it's urgent. It's about his mother."

Rachel jumped to her feet. "I won't take any more of your time, Dave. Thanks for your help."

She put her hand out, and he grasped it. "You will tell him, won't you?"

She nodded. "Yes. Yes, I will. And thanks again." Determination marking her stride, Rachel walked out of the office and waiting room and onto the street outside. Dave was right. She had to tell Mac. She could see that. But she wished there was some other way of accomplishing the same thing.

Dave pushed the lighted button on his phone. "Yes, Mike. What is it?"

"It's Mom."

Fear stabbed at Dave. "What's happened?"

"No, I didn't mean that, Dr. Gilchrist. I mean, Mom's okay. Or I think she is. But she's locked herself in her bedroom, and I can't get her to come out. I'm calling you because I didn't know who else to turn to. I mean who else she'd listen to. Could you please come help?"

"Yes, I'll come."

"How soon?"

Dave glanced at his appointments pad. "I'll come right now. And while you're waiting for me, try to keep your mother talking to you. Okay?"

There was a gasp at the other end of the line. "You don't think she'll . . ." Michael left the sentence unfinished.

"Mike, I don't know what to think. Just try to keep her talking, and I'll get right over there."

Cradling the phone, Dave said to the nurse,

"Explain to Mrs. Evans that I've been called out on an emergency, and either reschedule her or ask her to wait. The same with Mrs. Polonofski." They were his only two remaining appointments. "I'll call you as soon as I know when I'll be back."

"Yes, doctor," she said.

He slipped out the side door and headed for his car. In ten minutes he was at the Randolph house. Mike had apparently been watching for him out an upstairs window. He was at the door before Dave had a chance to ring the bell.

The young man was white-faced with worry. "I'm so glad you're here."

Striding past him into the foyer and up the stairs, Dave said, "Has she been talking to you?"

"A little."

"Then she hasn't taken anything." He had brought his black bag with him just in case. For all he knew, he might still need it.

"No, I don't think so," Mike said, hurrying after him.

At the top of the stairs Dave turned to him. "Maybe you'd better let me handle this."

"Sure, doctor. Whatever you say." He pointed down the hall. "That's her room there." He started back down the stairs. "I'll wait for you down in the living room."

"Okay, Mike. And thanks for calling me." Turning, Dave walked down the hall to the locked bedroom. "Pat," he called out to her, "it's Dave. Pat?"

A pause and then her voice. "Yes, I hear you."

"Will you let me talk to you?"

Another pause. A long one.

"Whatever it is, you'll have to face up to it sometime. You might as well start now. Please let me in."

In a moment or two he heard the key turn in the lock. He waited for her to open the door, but when she didn't he opened it and went inside the bedroom. She was standing halfway across the room, looking drained, her normally elegant blond hair mussed, her face whiter than Mike's had been.

Dave walked over to her. "Are you all right?"

"No, I wouldn't say that." Tears came into her eyes. She turned away from him.

He reached out and, taking her wrist, turned her gently back to him. "You haven't taken any pills or anything?"

She shook her head. "No. I—" She broke off.

He pressed the hand he still held. "What happened, Pat?"

She shrugged away from him, walked a few paces, and told him, with her back to him, what she had seen earlier that afternoon in her husband's office. "I guess," she finished, turning to face him, "there isn't going to be any reconciliation."

He had never seen such sadness on a person's face, and his heart went out to her. What a rotten thing for her to have stumbled on.

"I guess," she said, "I'd have to say our marriage is finished."

"I'm afraid so," he said as gently as he could.

Tears started at her eyes again, and again she

turned away from him until, he supposed, she could get herself in control.

After a few minutes she turned back to him, her eyes red-rimmed. "But there's more to it than that, Dave. I wish there wasn't, but there is. I have to talk to Barbara."

She flinched even as she said it. Dave frowned. "Why do you have to talk to her?"

"Because John lied to her. He told her that he and I had reached an amicable separation agreement, and that's a lie. We haven't reached any agreement of any kind. Only two days ago John told me there wasn't another woman in the picture, and when I asked him if he wanted a divorce he practically shouted at me that he didn't." A bit of spirit came into her voice. "Does that sound to you like an amicable separation agreement?"

Dave shook his head. "No. I don't understand him."

"You're not the only one." She sighed and flinched again. "But I have to tell Barbara."

"No." Dave put a hand up. "I can spare you that. I'll tell her."

She frowned. "Do you know her?"

"No. But that's no problem."

Pat looked relieved and distressed both at the same time. "I can't ask you to do this for me."

"You're not asking me," he said. "I'm volunteering." Again he put a hand up. "And no more objections. You're in no shape to talk to Barbara. As soon as I get back to the office I'll call her." He studied Pat's face. "The main thing I want to know is if you're all right, at least all right enough that you can cope."

After a moment she nodded. "Yes, I'm okay. Enough to cope anyhow, as you put it."

"Will you talk to Mike and let him know you're okay now?"

She nodded. "Yes, I'll talk to him. Tell him I'll be down in a few minutes. I just want to wash my face and comb my hair and—well, you know."

"If you need me for anything later on, will you call me?"

"Yes. And thanks, Dave."

"Don't mention it. In any event, I'll call you after I've spoken to Barbara."

He patted her shoulder and went downstairs to report to Mike, then called his office nurse to say he was on his way. And on the way back, he wondered over and over what kind of game John Randolph thought he was playing.

Rachel was back to trying to decide what to do. All the way home she had told herself she would tell Mac the truth.

But once home she wavered. Yes, she had promised Dave. But keeping promises had never been very high on her list, especially when there were extenuating circumstances. And there certainly were plenty of those.

She would of course tell Mac to stop feeling he was responsible for her miscarriage. That was ridiculous. He was in no way to blame.

That would take care of that problem. And as for

Iris . . . Rachel took in a deep breath and let it out again. Instead of telling Mac what Iris had done, she would use the information a better way.

She went to the phone and dialed Iris's number, heard several rings and then the click of somebody answering the phone.

"Hello." Iris herself.

"Iris, it's Rachel."

"Oh. Yes, dear. Have you decided?"

For a second she thought Iris had somehow read her mind or found out something on her own, but then she realized what Iris meant. "Oh, you mean about the studio."

"Yes, dear, of course." It was hard for Iris not to sound condescending, and she sounded it now.

"No. It's not the studio I'm calling about. It's about something else."

"Oh?" Iris sounded interested, but only barely.

"I'd like to come see you if it's all right with you."

"Well, yes. When did you have in mind?"

"Now?"

"No, not right now, dear. I'm doing my nails. Could you come over in an hour or so?"

"I guess I could," Rachel answered.

"I don't suppose," Iris added, "you want to give me a hint of what this is all about?"

Rachel was beginning to be irritated. Doing her nails indeed, as if she couldn't put that off or talk to Rachel while she was doing them. "All I can say, Iris, is that it's important."

Iris drew a little breath. "And I suppose I'll have

to be satisfied with that." She was back to sounding bored.

"Yes," Rachel said. "I'll see you in an hour or so."

Well, Rachel thought, after she'd said good-bye and hung up the phone, *you may be bored now, Iris, but after I get through talking to you, you won't be.*

And she allowed herself a small smile of anticipation. For once she was going to get the best of Iris.

Chapter Nine
Confrontations

"I have a call for you from Dr. David Gilchrist," Gloria said over the phone.

Perplexed, Barbara repeated his name. "Dr. David Gilchrist?" It wasn't that she'd never heard of him. She knew he was an internist connected to Bay City Memorial Hospital. But what did he want with her? "I don't understand," she said.

"What he wants, you mean?" Gloria asked. "Do you want me to find out?"

"No. I'll talk to him. Put him on, Gloria." The phone clicked. "Yes?" Barbara said.

"Miss Weaver, my name is Dave Gilchrist."

Before he could say more, Barbara cut in. "Yes, I know who you are. What I don't know is why you're calling me."

"Fair enough," he said. "I'm calling you to say I'd like to meet you and talk to you. And not," he added, "with any ulterior motives."

Well, she thought, that takes care of that idea. "I

appreciate your frankness, doctor, and I'd like to oblige you, but we have a court case beginning the first thing tomorrow, and I'm really awfully pressed for time just now. Could we put this off awhile?"

"No, I'm afraid we can't. It isn't just that I would like to meet you and talk to you. I must."

A faint feeling of foreboding crept up her backbone. She shivered. "Well, could you give me some idea of what this is all about?"

"Yes. I'm a friend of Pat and John Randolph. Though it would probably be more accurate at this point to say that Pat is feeling more friendly to me than John is."

The feeling of foreboding grew in strength. "I see." Before she could say more, John walked into her office, a sheaf of papers in his hand. "Could you hold on a moment, please?" Barbara said into the phone.

"Yes. Certainly," the doctor said.

"Darling," John said, "I didn't know you were on the phone. Forgive me."

"That's all right," she said. "What can I do for you?"

"Nothing now. Go back to your conversation. When you're finished, come into my office, will you?"

She nodded, and with a wave of his hand he walked out.

"I'm sorry," Barbara said into the phone. "You were saying?"

"That I have to talk to you. And the sooner the better."

"All right." She glanced at her desk calendar. "I'm all tied up this afternoon, I'm afraid."

"Could you meet me for a drink after you get off work?"

She hesitated, then said, "Yes, I guess I could do that."

"Do you have any preference as to where to meet?"

"No. It doesn't matter to me." The feeling of foreboding was now so strong she could barely contain it. "There's a cocktail lounge in the Beverly Hotel near here. It's quiet."

"All right," he said. "I'll meet you there. At five-fifteen?"

"Yes. That will be fine." She looked down at herself. "I'm wearing a dark blue suit with a light blue blouse. And I'm a blonde."

"I'll find you," he said. "Good-bye, Miss Weaver."

"Good-bye, doctor."

Barbara cradled her phone and sat staring at it, wondering what he had to see her about that was so urgent. Maybe Pat had changed her mind about the separation agreement. But why would she send this doctor to do her talking for her? And why was the doctor coming to her? Why wouldn't he talk to John about it?

With a shake of her head Barbara got up from her desk. She could spend the rest of the afternoon speculating and still come up with nothing. She went to John's office.

"You wanted me?"

He stood up from his desk and smiled at her. "Desperately."

She smiled back at him, some of her unsettling doubts washing away. Maybe Pat had had nothing to do with the doctor's call to her. Maybe the doctor was a busybody type who had called her all on his own because he hated seeing Pat and John split up.

John came around the desk, the sheaf of papers in his hand. "I thought you'd want to see these."

She took them from him. They were copies of financial records subpoenaed by the court. Looking at them, she shook her head over them.

"I think this gives our case a tremendous boost," he said.

Barbara nodded. "Yes. I agree with you. Anything else?" she asked, handing him the papers.

"Yes. Will you have dinner with me tonight?"

She smiled. "I think that could be arranged. What time?"

"I'm going to be stuck here in my office until about seven o'clock. Does that suit you?"

"Yes." She was tempted to tell him about her call from Dr. Gilchrist, but something held her back. Why not wait and see what the meeting with him was all about and then talk to John about it? "Well," she said, "I'd better get back to my own office."

She turned to go, but he put a hand on her wrist. "Don't go." His voice was husky.

Looking at him, feeling his touch, desire for him stirring in her, she decided her first hunch had been the right one: Pat had changed her mind and wanted him back. Barbara didn't blame her. Who wouldn't want him?

John pulled her to him and bent to kiss her, his mouth hungry on hers. She tried to pull away, but he wouldn't let her, indeed drew her more tightly to him until she was dizzy with desire, was kissing him with the same passionate intensity with which he was kissing her.

Where it would have ended she didn't know, but somebody came into the outer office, and they broke away from each other. Before anything more could be said or done Barbara fled from him to the safety of her own office, closing the door after her.

She sat down at her desk to regain her composure. It took several minutes, but she satisfied herself finally with the knowledge that she and John would be together, really together, after dinner tonight.

Rachel had long been a believer in looks. She hadn't always been able to afford the outfits she admired, but she could now, and before she went to see Iris she very carefully selected what she would wear.

She chose a demure outfit in pale green with a close-fitting skirt and bodice topped by a large white collar. Looking at herself in the mirror she added a strand of pearls that Mac had given her, and that Iris herself had coveted. With a pat of her hand on her dark hair she smiled at her reflection in the mirror. Then she left the house and drove to the Delaney home.

Iris met her at the door. "Come in, Rachel."

Iris had also dressed for the occasion, or so it seemed to Rachel. She was looking very elegant in black and white checkered linen accented by a thin black belt. But, then, Rachel couldn't recall ever seeing Iris when she didn't look elegant. Remembering how bored she had sounded on the phone an hour or so ago, Rachel doubted that she was the reason for the elegant outfit.

Rachel smiled as she walked into Iris's living room, feeling buoyant, really buoyant, thinking of all the times she'd been under Iris's thumb. Well, no more. This round was going to be hers.

And the pearls weren't lost on Iris either. "I see you're wearing the pearls Daddy gave you."

Rachel fingered them. "Yes. You know what they say about pearls."

Sitting on her sofa, waving Rachel to a chair, Iris put on a blank look. "No, dear. What do they say about them?"

"You have to wear them if you want them to keep their luster. Because of what your skin does for them."

"How very interesting," she said in such a listless way that Rachel wouldn't have been surprised if Iris had yawned. Rachel's feeling of buoyancy changed to steeliness.

"But I didn't come here to talk about pearls," she said.

Iris nodded. "No, I didn't suppose you had. And you said it isn't about the studio."

"No. Well, yes, it is in a way. I'm going to say no to the studio, Iris."

"I'm sorry to hear that. When it was such a lovely idea."

"Yes. Until I found out why you wanted to give it to me."

Iris looked bewildered, but Rachel figured it was probably a put-on look. "I don't understand what you mean," she said.

Not much you don't, Rachel thought. "Then I'll explain it, Iris. I didn't just dream I called you on the phone the night I miscarried. I really did call you."

Iris sighed. It was probably a put-on sigh to go with her put-on bewilderment. "I can't believe we're back to that. I thought we had it all worked out. You started to call me, maybe even got as far as the telephone to call me, but then—"

"I did call you, Iris," Rachel interrupted. "Tracey DeWitt was here in the house with you when I called that night, and she says I called you. Now do you still want to deny it?"

A wary look was on Iris's face now. "Have you been talking to Tracey?"

"No," Rachel said, and said no more than that. Let Iris think for a moment or two that she had made all this up about Tracey.

And she was thinking it. Rachel could see that in her face. "Then how do you know where Tracey was or wasn't that night?"

"Because she wrote it down on a piece of paper."

Iris frowned. "What piece of paper?"

"A piece of paper she gave to somebody to hold on to."

"What person?"

"What difference does it make what person?" She wasn't about to name John Randolph. Who knew what Iris might do to get back at him.

Iris made a face. "If you won't name the person it's because you can't name the person. Meaning there isn't anybody to name. Meaning you're making all of this up."

"I'm sure that's what you'd like to think, Iris. But there is a person, and there is a piece of paper, and it's full of Tracey DeWitt's big, splashy handwriting."

The look on Iris's face changed again. The description of Tracey's handwriting had probably done it.

"And," Rachel went on, "there's more in her handwriting than just the business of my making the phone call here that night. There's the whole business about you and Robert and Clarice's baby."

In reading magazine stories Rachel had often wondered what the writers meant when they said somebody's face darkened. Now she knew.

"I don't believe you," Iris said, clenching her fists.

Rachel shrugged. "Well, believe me or don't, Iris. But we both know what Tracey said is true. So that part of it doesn't matter. It doesn't matter to me, and it shouldn't matter to you. What should matter to you is what I'm going to do with the information."

Iris looked as if she'd rather bite her tongue off, but after a bit of a struggle she asked. Coldly. As if her manner showed she was only asking to keep the conversation going, not because she cared. "And what are you going to do with it?"

Rachel let her sweat it out a moment or two. Then she shrugged again. "That all depends on you. I could go to Mac and tell him everything and let him decide what to do. In fact, I've been advised to do exactly that."

"Advised by whom?"

"I don't see that that matters, either. Let's just say it was somebody who has my welfare in mind, and Mac's. Did you know that Mac thinks he's to blame for my losing the baby?"

"No, I didn't know that." For once she sounded genuine, but it didn't last. She drew herself up and said, "That's ridiculous."

"Yes," Rachel said, nodding. "Of course it's ridiculous. If anybody is to blame for my miscarriage, it's you."

Iris now looked horrified, and that was probably genuine, too.

"That's why the person advised me to tell Mac the truth about the phone call," Rachel continued, "so he can stop feeling guilty."

Iris said nothing.

"I didn't know until today that Mac feels he was to blame. I knew something was bothering him, but he wouldn't tell me what. He wouldn't even admit to it. But now that I do know, I can talk it out with him, tell him to stop feeling guilty." She spread her hands. "And I can do that without telling him about the phone call."

She sat back in her chair and waited for Iris to

156

say something. It was a long wait, but finally Iris gave in. "And what am I supposed to say to that?"

"Is that what you want me to do, Iris? Not tell Mac about the phone call?"

A look of hatred came into Iris's eyes, such naked hatred that Rachel flinched. "All right, Rachel," she said in an icy voice. "And what do I do for you in return? I assume there is a return here."

Rachel smiled. In the face of all that hatred she not only smiled, she made it one of her best ones. "That's right, Iris. Yes. There is a return, and it's a very simple one. From here on out you stay away from Mac and me. Completely away. If you don't, then I will tell him."

All of Iris's pent-up emotion burst out of her at hearing that. She jumped to her feet, her fists clenched again. "You can't do that to me. That's blackmail!"

Rachel answered the outburst with another shrug. "Yes," she said, "I suppose it is."

Iris was still fuming. "Well, you're not going to get away with it, Rachel, because I won't let you."

Slowly and carefully, as if she were favoring a weak ankle, Rachel got up from the chair. Turning to Iris she offered her another smile. "You can scream and fume and carry on to your heart's content, but those are the terms. You stay away from your father and me, you have nothing further to do with either one of us, and I'll keep silent about the phone call. But one word or one move out of you, and I tell Mac everything. Including the part about you and Robert and Clarice and her

157

baby." Rachel smoothed her pale green skirt. "You can stay where you are, Iris. I can see myself out."

And out she went with not so much as a glance behind her.

Barbara walked into the cocktail lounge of the Beverly Hotel, blinking into the semidarkness after the bright sun outside. A youngish man at a table not far from the entrance stood up. "Miss Weaver?" he said.

"Yes." She walked over to him, her hand outstretched. "Dr. Gilchrist?"

He shook hands with her. "Yes. Won't you sit down?" He held her chair for her, then sat back down across the table from her. "What would you like to drink?"

She didn't know that she wanted to drink anything, but she said, "A glass of white wine, I guess."

He ordered the same for both of them, then waited until the wine was brought and the waiter departed before speaking.

"I don't want to waste your time beating around the bush," he said after taking a sip of his wine. "Nor do I want to be so blunt as to seem unduly cruel."

The familiar feeling of foreboding came rushing back. Barbara gestured with her hand. "Say what you have to say, doctor. I'm a big girl."

"I understand John told you he and Pat had made a separation agreement."

Barbara nodded. "Yes. An amicable one."

He took another sip. "Well, unfortunately, Miss

Weaver, that's not true. There's been no separation agreement, amicable or otherwise."

Barbara stared at him in disbelief. "But I don't understand. Why would John tell me there was one if there wasn't?"

Dave sighed. "I wish I could answer that question, Miss Weaver, but I can't. I don't know what kind of game John has been playing with you, but let me tell you the rest of it."

"Go on," she said, unable to imagine what more there could be, still struggling to understand why John had lied to her. What was the point of it?

"Over the weekend," Dr. Gilchrist was saying, "Saturday afternoon, as I recall, Pat went to John's apartment to ask for a reconciliation. It was a rather heated confrontation, but when Pat asked John if there was somebody else in his life, some other woman he was interested in, he denied it."

Barbara was now staring at him openmouthed.

"I'm sorry," he said. "I hate to be doing this to you. Obviously you had no notion about any of this."

"None," she managed to get out.

"Pat didn't believe John when he said there was nobody else, so she said she would go to a lawyer about getting a divorce, but he told her not to do that. He didn't want a divorce."

Aware that she was still staring at the doctor, and aware, too, that her face was flushed, Barbara took a sip of her wine and nearly choked on it. Setting the glass down, clearing her throat, she said, "I'm sorry, but I just—I just . . ." Her voice trailed off. She didn't know what to say or do. She was devastated. How could John have done this to her? And why? What had she ever done to him to deserve this? Her silly little impulsive invitation to come home with her that time? Could that have brought all this upon her?

Barbara shook her head, unable to believe it.

And there was something more, if only she could gather her poor scattered wits together. Yes. How did Pat know that John had lied to her? He surely wouldn't have admitted doing so.

"Dr. Gilchrist," she said, "how did Pat know that John had lied to me?"

"She went to his office early this afternoon to ask him again for a reconciliation. His secretary was not in the outer office, and when she went into John's office, you and he were there together."

Barbara was back to staring at him. "Oh, Lord," she said, recalling. "She saw us kissing."

"And she heard the conversation between you about the separation agreement."

"Oh, Lord," Barbara said again, feeling worse than before if that was possible. "Oh, what must she think of me? I had no idea."

Hearing herself say that, she wasn't sure it made any sense, but Dave nodded. "Pat thinks you've been taken for a ride, to put it rather bluntly."

"I had no idea," Barbara said again. "John was so reassuring about Pat. I mean, about her not standing in the way. Oh, Lord. I never would have—" She broke off with a shake of her head. "The more I talk, the deeper the hole I dig for myself."

"I'm sorry," Dr. Gilchrist said.

Barbara looked at him. He probably couldn't think of anything else to say. And what a nasty mission he had undertaken. For Pat probably, rather than make her have to do it herself. John wouldn't have owned up to all this on his own.

She shook her head again. She couldn't get over John doing this to her. And for what? A few happy times together? Because that's all it would ever have been. Sooner or later, for the sake of her pride she hoped sooner, she would have begun pressing John to sue for a divorce from Pat or get Pat to sue for a divorce from him so that she and John could get on with their lives.

She must have looked as devastated as she felt, because Dr. Gilchrist said, "Would you like me to see you home?"

She shook her head. "No, thank you. It's very kind of you, but—"

"It's no trouble, Miss Weaver. I'd be happy to do it."

"You don't understand. I'm not going home. I'm supposed to go back to the office to meet John. We were going to have dinner together. Now of course I—" She broke off. "Well, I'll have it out with him."

"I'm sorry," Dr. Gilchrist said again.

"Yes, I know. I'm sorry, too. I—I want to tell you I appreciate your telling me."

"I didn't enjoy doing it."

"No. I can see that."

He finished his wine. "Well, I can at least see you to the door of your office building."

He signaled the waiter for the check and paid the bill. Then they left the cocktail lounge together and set off for the building a couple of blocks away.

At the revolving door he said, "I wish you well, Miss Weaver."

It seemed a curious thing to say, but she supposed he felt he had to say something positive. "Thank you," she responded. "And good night."

"Good night."

She pushed on the door panel and went inside the building. She would have given almost anything not to have to go up to the office, but she had no choice.

Chapter Ten
Resolutions

Robert Delaney came home from the office that same evening determined to ask Iris for a divorce. There was practically nothing left of their marriage, and why spend any more of his life married to a woman he didn't love?

He was a good-looking man, with dark curly hair and a jaunty, dashing air about him. He was used to regarding himself as young, but only this afternoon one of the new secretaries in the office had addressed him as Mr. Delaney in the tone of voice such sweet young things reserved for men they regarded as old. A probe in the mirror of the men's room had confirmed his having thinning hair, perhaps giving rise to the determination to ask Iris for a divorce.

Whatever had precipitated it was swept away by the storm that confronted him when he reached home. Iris met him at the door wild-eyed, her face streaked with tears, her usually perfect coiffure mussed, her usually carefully applied makeup smeared, her black and white linen dress rumpled.

"What's the matter?" he asked, frowning. "What's happened?"

"It's Rachel," she said, spitting the words out and clenching her fists. "Oh, why did she have to come into my life? Why?"

"Calm down," Robert said. "Let me fix you a drink." He walked ahead of her into the living room, went to the bar set up at the end of it, and turned around to her. "What would you like?"

She shook her head. "I don't want anything. I'm too upset to have a drink."

"Well," he said, turning back to the bar, reaching for the bottle of scotch, "I'm not." He poured himself a drink, added ice, and stirred it, then took an appreciative swallow. "All right," he said, turning back again to her, "now tell me what happened."

"Rachel was just here."

He shrugged. "So I gather. What did she want?"

"What does Rachel ever want? The rest of the world to do her bidding." She clenched her fists again. "Well, I'm not going to do it, and there's no way she can make me, either."

"Iris," Robert said, "you're talking in circles. What exactly did Rachel want?"

"She came here to tell me I couldn't see my daddy anymore."

He frowned. "Why?"

"What does it matter why?"

"What do you mean, what does it matter why?

She had to have had some reason for such a sweeping statement as that. What's been going on between the two of you?"

Iris sat down on the sofa, her body going limp in a way that seemed to spell defeat. "Nothing's been going on between us," she said.

He shook his head. "Are you saying that Rachel came over here and for no reason whatsoever told you you couldn't see your father anymore?"

"Yes."

He took another swallow of his drink. "I don't believe it."

Iris made a sour face. "That's right," she said, a show of spirit returning to her voice, "take her side against me."

"I'm not taking any side," he answered her. "As far as I've been able to figure out, there isn't any side to take." He took another swallow of his drink, the scotch beginning to take effect now, relaxing him.

"She hates me," Iris said, venom in her voice now, her body stiffening. "She's always trying to drive my father and me apart."

"If you ask me," Robert said, "I'd say it was just the opposite. You're always trying to drive your father and Rachel apart."

"He never should have married her."

"Maybe so, but he did. And he seems quite happy with her."

Iris turned away from him in a gesture of contempt. "Oh, what's the good of talking to you?"

He shrugged. "None, I expect. But look at it this

way. If you can't talk to your father, and apparently you can't, who else have you got?"

If that had been an attempt on his part to calm her, and he wasn't so sure it was, it didn't work. "Oh," she said, "you make me sick."

He raised his half-empty glass in a halfhearted toast to her. "The feeling is mutual. I suppose," he added, "I could call Rachel and ask her what this is all about."

Iris gave him a black look. "You wouldn't dare."

He arched his eyebrows. "Wouldn't I? Is that your explanation for not explaining what was behind Rachel's coming here—because you also don't dare?"

She didn't answer him.

"I expect it is," he said, answering himself. "Whatever Rachel's reason, I expect it was a good one. She doesn't go out of her way to make trouble for herself."

"You stay out of this," Iris warned.

"Out of what? I'm still waiting for you to tell me that."

"Never mind. Just stay out of it."

Robert finished his drink and turned back to the bar to pour another. "I'm not making any promises of any kind," he said.

The second drink was even more relaxing than the first, partly because it was the second drink, and partly because Robert took it into his den to savor it away from Iris and whatever was bugging her.

Whatever it was, he couldn't bring up the subject of divorce until this other business was settled. Iris would simply wave any discussion aside.

That meant this other business had to be settled, and the sooner, the better.

He put down his drink and picked up the telephone. About to call Rachel, he changed his mind. She probably wouldn't tell him anything, either. Better to call Mac. Nodding in agreement with himself, he dialed Mac's office. The switchboard put him through.

"Mac Cory, please," he said to the secretary. "This is Robert Delaney calling."

"I'm sorry, Mr. Delaney," she said. "He isn't here."

"Can you tell me where I can reach him?"

"He's out on a story and can't be reached," she said.

Robert frowned. "Do you expect him back soon?"

"Within the hour. Shall I have him call you?"

"Yes, please. Tell him I'm at home," Robert said. Thanking her, he cradled the phone and picked up his drink again. Whatever had happened between Rachel and Iris, Mac would settle one way or the other.

John was putting the finishing touches on the opening statement he would deliver in the courthouse case. He glanced at his watch. He was making better time than he had expected. As soon as Barbara got back from wherever it was she had gone, they could go out to dinner and let the evening proceed from there.

The sound of the key in the outer office door made him look up from his notes, then get up and start out to greet her.

"Darling," he said as she came through the door, "I was hoping—" At sight of the grim expression on her face he broke off, frowning. "Barbara, what's the matter? What's happened? Are you all right?"

Closing the outer door behind her, she shook her head. "No, I'm not all right, and neither are you, John."

He stared at her, bewildered. "I don't know what you mean."

She didn't explain immediately but stood there for a few moments staring at him. "What I don't understand," she said at last, "is why you lied to me, why you told me you and Pat had agreed to part when there was no such agreement at all."

"Who have you been talking to?" he asked, not because it mattered but as to have something to say.

"I've been talking to David Gilchrist," she said. "But only because he wanted to spare Pat the ordeal of doing it. Pat came here this afternoon to ask you once again to reconcile with her. She found us in here together."

John said nothing, knowing there was nothing he could say.

Barbara walked past him toward her office, and he followed her. She started emptying her desk drawers, piling papers and pens and pencils on the top of the desk.

168

"What are you doing?" he asked.

"What it looks like I'm doing," she answered. "Getting out of here."

"But, Barbara," he remonstrated, "you don't have to—"

She put up a hand to stop him in midsentence. "If you're saying I don't have to leave, that I don't have to quit my job, then save your breath. I'm quitting. There's no way I could stay on here and work with you after the way you betrayed me."

She was right, of course. "I'm sorry," he said.

She stopped emptying the desk drawers long enough to search his face. "Are you? Are you really sorry?"

He felt the blood rush to his face, and he was at a loss for words again.

She went back to her task, and he watched her, wishing none of this was real, though he should have known all along, and probably had, that something like this was bound to have happened.

"And it isn't only me you betrayed," she said after a few moments. "You betrayed Pat, as well."

"Yes," he said, "I know that."

Once again Barbara stopped what she was doing to search his face. "Why, John? Did either Pat or I deserve to be treated like that?"

"No."

"Then, why?"

He couldn't meet her searching gaze and looked away. "I don't know. I don't have any excuses. And, Barbara, I *am* sorry. Please believe that."

With a shake of her head, she opened another

drawer. "I don't know what to believe. Except what a monumental fool I've been. I can believe that with no trouble at all."

For a few minutes he watched her in silence. "I wish you'd reconsider quitting your job. I promise I'll stay away from you."

She didn't so much as pause in taking her belongings out of the desk. "No, John. Even if I wanted to stay, and I don't, I couldn't add to Pat's suffering by doing that. It's best all around, for all of us, for me to clear out of here."

The bottom drawer of her desk had some empty shopping bags in it. She got them out and packed her things in them. There were law books among the papers and personal belongings, so they had to be heavy.

"Let me help you downstairs with them," he said when she had finished.

"I don't need your help and I don't want it." She dug a ring of keys out of her purse. Slipping the office keys off, she put them on the desk top. "There are your keys." She gathered the shopping bags together, two in one hand, three in the other.

"Barbara," he said, "at least let me carry some of those bags."

She shook her blond head. "No. If you'll just get out of the way, please."

He stood aside, and she wobbled past him, the shopping bags weighing her down.

"Where will you go?" he said, starting after her.

"When I find out," she answered, not turning around to him, "I'll let Gloria know."

"I'm sorry," he said again.

She didn't turn to answer, continuing to walk out of the office and down the hall to the elevators.

He stood in the doorway until the elevator car had come and gone, then he went back to his own office. His notes were on his desk where he'd left them. Picking them up, he shoved them in his briefcase.

Doing that drew his eyes to his family's portrait. Sitting down at his desk, he picked it up and held it in his hands. What a fool he had been. And what a child, wanting to have his cake and eat it too.

He looked at the picture. Pat stared out at him, her eyes filled with love and pride.

He had never been worthy of her, had never deserved her. And what must she think of him now.

To think that only this afternoon she had come here still wanting to make things up with him. Was there a chance that, in spite of what she had seen here, she could forgive and forget?

He hardly dared think so.

But what did he have if he didn't have Pat?

He went on sitting at the desk, staring at her image, overcome with guilt and remorse. Eventually he put the picture back in its place, gathered up his things, and left the office. He would go to Pat to ask her forgiveness, to ask her to take him back, sinner or no.

Robert had finished his third scotch and was looking through an architectural magazine when the phone rang in the den. He answered it and was happy to hear Mac's voice.

"Hi, Mac. I called about Iris and Rachel."

There was a defensive edge in Mac's voice when he responded. "What about them? What's going on?"

"I don't know exactly," Robert said. "But Rachel was here this afternoon delivering an ultimatum."

This time there was disbelief in his father-in-law's voice. "Rachel? An ultimatum?"

"That's right."

"What about?"

"I don't know the whole of that either," Robert said. "Only that Rachel told Iris she was to stay away from the two of you from now on."

"But why?"

"I don't know. I tried to get it out of Iris, but she wouldn't tell me. But I can tell you she was upset with a capital U."

"Yes, I can imagine," Mac said. "Maybe I'd better talk to her. No," he added hastily, "I guess the person I should talk to is Rachel. I was about ready to leave here anyhow. I'll talk to her when I get home."

"Yes, do that," Robert said, "before things can get any worse than they are."

If that's possible, he added to himself when his telephone conversation was over, only half-believing that it was.

Pat Randolph had also spent some time on the phone, the most important call the one from Dave Gilchrist saying he had met with Barbara and had told her everything she needed to know about John.

172

"How did she take it?" Pat asked.

"She was stunned," Dave answered.

Pat nodded. "So she wasn't part of the game that was being played."

"No way," Dave said. "Not unless she's Sarah Bernhardt brought back to life."

"I never thought she was part of it," Pat said. "It wouldn't have been like her. Well, thanks for calling and telling me."

"I also called to see how you are," he said.

"I'm okay."

"Is Mike there with you?"

"No. He went back to his apartment. He offered to stay, but I told him I'm all right. And I am."

"Do you want me to come over?"

"No, thanks. To tell you the truth I'd rather be alone this evening. I have a lot of thinking to do. I do that best when I'm by myself."

"No more locking yourself in your bedroom."

"No. I'm past that."

"Good," he said. "I'm glad to hear it. If you change your mind, if the evening starts hanging heavy on you, will you give me a call?"

"Thanks, Dave, I will. And thank you more than I can say for meeting with Barbara for me."

Her phone call with Dave Gilchrist finished, Pat did what she had told him she was going to do. She curled up on the living room sofa and tried to think about John and Barbara and herself: what had happened, what was going to happen, what had been said, what still needed to be said.

She was startled when the doorbell rang, more startled still when she saw that it was Barbara at the door. She wasn't at all sure she wanted to see her and talk to her, but she invited her in, leading the way into the living room and gesturing her to a chair. She curled up again on the sofa herself, as if she were on the defense and needed the sofa's protection.

Barbara said, "It's good of you to see me, Pat. I—I feel terrible about what's happened."

"Yes," Pat agreed, "I'm sure you do."

"After I left Dr. Gilchrist I went back to the office and broke off with John. I—I couldn't believe he would do what he did. To you and to me." She shook her head. "I'm still having trouble believing it."

"I know," Pat said. "I feel the same way myself."

"I don't know what you must think of me. I mean, for getting involved with him in the first place. But you have to believe it would never have happened if I had known you still wanted him." She spread her hands. "Please believe that."

Pat put out a hand to her. "I do believe it. You've always been so open and up-front, I couldn't see you sneaking around as a third in a relationship."

"I guess that's partly why John behaved the way he did. Because I pressured him. I told him we couldn't have anything between us until things were straightened out between you and him."

Pat shook her head. "Don't blame yourself, Barbara. John is the one at fault here."

"Yes, I know. But I've always admired him. Even before—well, you know. So I guess I had to look for reasons for his doing what he did. A man doesn't step out of character overnight, yet that's what he seems to have done." She sighed. "I'm sorry all the way around. I wish being sorry did more to help than it does."

"I know what you mean. But times helps, Barbara."

She nodded. "I suppose. And I've quit my job with him."

Pat was surprised to hear that. "Have you?"

"Yes. John didn't want me to. Partly, I'm sure, because of the courthouse business coming to trial tomorrow. And I'm sorry if that leaves him in a bind, but there was no way I could go on working with him." She shook her head. "Not after all this."

The surprise Pat had felt dissipated. Of course Barbara couldn't go on working with him. Whether she loved him or despised him, she couldn't see him every day without putting herself through a lot of emotional turmoil. "But what will you do?" Pat asked.

"Get a job somewhere else," Barbara said. "But all I'm not worried about it. I've had a number of offers the last few months from law firms in different places. I had one just the other day from a firm in Gary, Indiana. So what I'll do is write to tell them all I'm now available and ask them to make me an offer." She shrugged. "One of them is bound to connect."

"I hope so," Pat said sincerely.

"Oh, I'm sure of it." Barbara smiled. "This is a

good time to be a lady lawyer. To be a lady anything in the workplace."

Pat nodded. "Will you let me know when you get located?"

A surprised look came into Barbara's eyes. "Do you really want to know?"

Pat nodded again.

"Then of course I will. And thank you."

She thought for a moment that Barbara was going to cry. Pat hoped desperately that she didn't, because if she did, then she would end up crying, too, and she'd done enough crying that day to last a lifetime.

Barbara didn't cry. She blinked a few times until she could get herself under control, then she stood up. "Well, I won't take up any more of your time." She put her hand out, and Pat stood up from the couch and grasped it. "Thank you more than I can ever say, Pat, for being so understanding."

Pat now had to blink her own eyes to keep herself from crying. She squeezed Barbara's hand and then quickly turned and led the way back to the front door. "Good-bye, Barbara. Thank you for coming to see me."

"Thank you for letting me." With a wave of her hand, Barbara turned and went down the walk to where her car was parked at the curb.

Pat stood in the doorway until the car disappeared down the street, then she went back inside the house and curled up on the couch again, alone with her thoughts.

Some time later the doorbell rang again.

Pat's first response was that Barbara had left something behind, but there was no evidence in the living room of that. Her second thought was that it was Marianne, home from her travels.

But it was John.

"May I come in?" he asked her.

She didn't know what to say, didn't know whether she wanted him to come in or not. She felt vulnerable, and she knew that was a dangerous way to feel. At length she nodded and held the door wider.

She let him lead the way. It was, after all, as much his house as hers, even though he hadn't been living here for a while.

He walked into the living room and she followed him. He sat in the big yellow armchair, his favorite. She curled up yet again on the sofa, the feeling even stronger now than it had been with Barbara that she needed all the defensive protection she could get. She waited for him to speak. He must have something to say to her. He had sought her out, not the other way around.

"I've been sitting in the office thinking," he began.

"That's what I've been doing here," she said, finding her voice.

"Have you come to any conclusions?" he asked softly.

She shrugged. "I don't know."

He sat silent for a few moments, then got up from the chair and prowled restlessly around the room, picking up a book from an end table, glancing at it, putting it back down, touching a flower in a vase, staring into the fireplace for a few minutes.

Standing with his back to her, he said, "I've been a terrible fool, Pat."

She frowned. What was she supposed to say to that? She couldn't disagree. She said nothing.

He turned around to her. "I never wanted to break off with you."

"Then, why did you?"

"Because I felt you had left me out of things."

"But we've been through all that, John."

"Yes, I know. And I know what you said about it. I mean, how you explained it." He turned around to stare into the fireplace again. "What I'm trying to say, Pat—and it isn't easy to say—is that I didn't intend for our breakup to be permanent." He turned back to her. "I only wanted you to get a taste of what I'd gotten. To feel the way I'd felt."

"I see."

"Do you?" He sounded desperate.

She said nothing because she didn't see, not really. For a grown-up man he sounded adolescent.

And there was more to it than that.

It took nerve to say it, but she did. "And what part did Barbara play in that?"

The question made him avert his gaze from her again. "She didn't play any part in it," he said. "I didn't mean to get involved with her. Truly I didn't. It just, well, it just happened."

"And did you also just happen to lie to her?"

To John's credit he turned back to her at that,

though he flinched as well. "I deserved that," he said. "I lied to her because she wouldn't have had anything to do with me otherwise. Pat," he added, coming toward her from across the room, "I'm trying to be honest with you."

"Yes, I know that."

"It isn't easy."

"I know that, too."

"I'm hoping you can forgive me."

And there it was. That was why he had come to see her—to ask her forgiveness and, once she had forgiven him, to ask her to take him back.

She had expected it. In fact, she had sat there on the sofa thinking about his doing what he now was doing.

She shook her head. "No, John. I'm sorry, but I can't."

He stared at her in disbelief. "But you must."

"You have a short memory."

"I don't know what you mean."

"Don't you? Do you remember how I came to your apartment last Saturday and asked you to forgive me?"

"Well, yes, but—"

"But what, John? But that was different? Is that what you were going to say?"

"No, of course not."

She shrugged. "Well, it doesn't matter. The point is you didn't forgive me, did you?"

"No, but . . ."

She cocked her head at him. "And there it is again. But. But what? But you meant to later on?

179

After I'd had a taste of my own medicine, is that it? After I'd had enough time to feel the way you felt? Left out, I think you said."

His face was flushed.

"And meanwhile," she continued, "you had Barbara to play with. To take your mind off your loneliness. You had a second wife—a substitute wife—to cook your meals and soothe your hurts and make love to."

"Don't," he said, putting a hand up. "Please don't, Pat."

Still curled up on the sofa, she stared up at him. "Why shouldn't I, John? Isn't that the truth? Isn't that part of why you weren't ready to forgive me Saturday? You had Barbara and didn't need me. And when you tired of Barbara, or when she began to put too much pressure on you, demanding to know why our divorce wasn't moving along faster, then you could break off with her, saying you'd had a change of heart, after all. You would tell her you were sorry if you'd led her down the garden path, that you hadn't really meant to. That you'd honestly believed that you and I were finished, but then when push came to shove you had discovered you hadn't wanted to divorce me, after all. Wasn't that how you were going to get out of it?"

He sighed. "I suppose so."

"And now you want me to forgive you."

He searched her face. "Yes, I do want that. Please, Pat. I know I've hurt you."

"And betrayed me."

He nodded.

"And refused to forgive me for my sins."

"Yes. That, too."

She looked at him incredulously. "And you still expect me to forgive you?"

He shook his head. "No, not expect. Just want."

For some moments she didn't say anything. She supposed she could forgive him. It was in her power. And then he would come back to her, and they would resume their marriage.

Except that Barbara would be there between them. That was what Pat couldn't forgive—that he had used Barbara to keep them estranged until it suited him to take her back.

Well, she didn't want him back on those terms. She would get no happiness out of it.

And what was a marriage for if it wasn't for happiness? Mutual happiness.

"No, John," she said, defeated. "I'm sorry. But I can't forgive you. You ended our marriage, and—"

He cut her off. "I didn't end it."

"Maybe not from your point of view you didn't, but you did from mine. You ended it and it's going to stay ended."

"Pat, I beg you."

"No, don't," she said. "I don't want that." She got up from the couch and headed toward the front door. "All I want is for you to leave." She stood at the front door, waiting for him to join her there.

Eventually he did, but he still wasn't taking no for an answer. "Pat," he said again miserably. "Please. Please take me back."

She shook her head. "No. I'm sorry, John. You could have prevented all this, but it's too late now. Good-bye."

"I won't say good-bye," he said.

"Then, just go."

And after a long and searching look at her, he left.

Rachel was still savoring the satisfaction of her encounter with Iris when Mac came home. She had all she could do not to greet him at the door with it, but then her first look at him drove it all out of her head. Something had happened.

"Mac," she said, alarmed, "what's happened?"

"That's what I came home to find out from you."

She stared at him in bewilderment. She couldn't believe Iris had phoned him or gone to see him. But what else could he be talking about?

They walked together into the living room.

"Robert called me a little while ago," he said, then proceeded to tell her what Robert had said.

So that was it.

He patted her hand. "I want to know what this is all about."

"Oh, Mac." She took his hand and squeezed it. "This isn't how I meant for it to go at all."

He searched her face.

"I meant for Iris to stay away from us. Leave us alone." She looked away from him.

He took her chin in his hand and turned her to him. "That was your ultimatum?"

She didn't like the word any better than she liked his question, but she had to answer it. "Yes."

"And what reason did you give her?"

"She told a lie about me."

"What lie?"

"Mac," she said, "can't we just let it go at that?"

"No, darling, you know we can't. I have to know what's going on here. What is it?"

Rachel took a deep breath and let it out. "The night I lost the baby. Iris said I only dreamed I called her at her house looking for you. But that was a lie. I did call her, and she said you were in the den talking to Robert and couldn't be disturbed, and then she hung up on me."

Mac's face flushed with fury, his eyes wide.

"I assumed it was something important," Rachel added, "so I didn't call back."

"Oh, yes," he said in a voice heavy with irony, "so important I can't even remember now what we were talking about."

"Anyhow," Rachel said, "the pains started getting worse, and I passed out, and then—" She spread her hands. "But you know all the rest of it."

"Yes," he said, getting up from where they were sitting together on the couch and starting to pace, something he always did when he was upset. "Including the fact that the baby could have been saved if only I'd gotten here sooner."

Rachel stood and went to him. "I was going to tell you that part of it, Mac. I mean, that it wasn't your fault I lost the baby."

"No, I can see that now. It was Iris's fault." He picked up an ashtray from the side table and threw it across the room into the fireplace, causing Rachel to jump as it shattered into tiny shards of crystal. "Damn the woman and her interfering. Why couldn't she have let me talk to you?"

Rachel swallowed. She had never seen Mac so

furious. "I don't know. I only know Iris has always done everything she can think of to drive us apart."

"Well, that's finished now. And so are Iris and me. I'll tell you something, Rachel. In fact, I'll make you a promise. And that is I'll never see Iris again. Never."

Rachel gasped. It was all too much to hope for. "Do you mean that, Mac?"

"Yes, I do." He put a hand up. "No. Wait a minute. I'll have to see her one last time." He glanced at his watch. "And I'll do it now."

Rachel put a hand on his arm, fearing the ominous tone of his voice. "Wait, Mac. Do you want to see her when you're this upset? Don't you think maybe you should wait until you've had time to cool down a bit?"

He brushed her hand aside. "No. I'll do it now. I want to be upset. I want her to see exactly what her lies and her schemes have done. I want to give her a firsthand demonstration of it."

He turned and left the house, the door slamming after him. Rachel remained standing where she was, shivering. She had always wanted Iris out of her life, always wanted Mac to forsake his daughter. Could her wish be coming true? And if it was, at what cost to her own happiness?